THE SENATOR'S CHILDREN

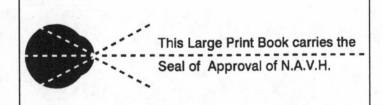

This Large Print Book carries the
Seal of Approval of N.A.V.H.

THE SENATOR'S CHILDREN

NICHOLAS MONTEMARANO

THORNDIKE PRESS
A part of Gale, a Cengage Company

GALE
A Cengage Company

Farmington Hills, Mich • San Francisco • New York • Waterville, Maine
Meriden, Conn • Mason, Ohio • Chicago

Copyright © 2017 by Nicholas Montemarano.
Thorndike Press, a part of Gale, a Cengage Company.

ALL RIGHTS RESERVED
Thorndike Press® Large Print Reviewer's Choice.
The text of this Large Print edition is unabridged.
Other aspects of the book may vary from the original edition.
Set in 16 pt. Plantin.

**LIBRARY OF CONGRESS CIP DATA ON FILE.
CATALOGUING IN PUBLICATION FOR THIS BOOK
IS AVAILABLE FROM THE LIBRARY OF CONGRESS**

ISBN-13: 978-1-4328-4783-8 (hardcover)
ISBN-10: 1-4328-4783-x (hardcover)

Published in 2018 by arrangement with Tin House Books

Printed in Mexico
1 2 3 4 5 6 7 22 21 20 19 18

"A line can be straight, or a street, but the human heart, oh, no, it's curved like a road through mountains."

— TENNESSEE WILLIAMS

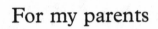

For my parents

■ ■ ■ ■

PART ONE:
SYMPATHY VOTE

1984–1985

■ ■ ■ ■

OCTOBER 23, 1984

Danielle Christie wasn't hoping that her husband would lose, but she wouldn't be sad when it was over. It would be over soon — that is, if polls were even close to accurate. She didn't like playing the role of candidate's wife; she was just an academic. She certainly didn't like attending events and tried to stay away from the campaign as much as possible. But David couldn't be in two places at once, and there was low-hanging fruit ripe for the taking, as David's people put it, and he had asked Danielle to attend a fundraiser on his behalf.

She knew what to do: smile, be charming, make nice, say the right things, don't say the wrong things, stay on message, talk about what a great husband and father David was, how they'd met in college, how he'd dropped Modern Drama, Danielle's favorite class, but kept reading the plays just

11

so he could talk with her about them. People loved that story. But inside she was always dying a little at these events. She would rather be home in her robe and slippers reading *Amadeus* or *The Elephant Man*. A glass of wine. Maybe two.

Late October, a fundraiser on the Main Line. A mansion right out of *The Philadelphia Story*. Deep pockets. Old money. Low-hanging fruit. David's flight from Pittsburgh would get in a few hours too late for him to make it, and someone had to be there. So Danielle asked the sitter to watch Betsy until David arrived home and took Nick with her. She'd brought him to a few fundraisers before. He was sixteen and looked like his father. He was naturally charming; no need for *him* to fake it.

Soon, she kept thinking, we can go back to normal. She didn't like thinking that way, she knew how David hated to lose, but double digits two weeks out — it would take a miracle.

She drove down a long driveway to the front entrance, where one staff member took the car to park it and another led them into a grand foyer, up a sweeping staircase, and into a sitting room where everything was white — white chairs, white sofas, white fainting couch, white people. The guests applauded when Danielle and Nick walked into the room as if they'd done something worthy of applause. It helped to have Nick there, to be able to introduce him to people, let *him* be the center of attention, he didn't mind, or to watch him across the room, already so comfortable in the world of adults.

People were talking, she could see their mouths moving, but she didn't really hear them. Why was it so hot? Why were there three fireplaces in the room? She imagined that everyone might disappear except her and Nick. She might enjoy her glass of wine — her second already — and ask Nick about the Stephen King novel he was reading, *Pet Sematary.* Any book that deliberately misspelled a word in the title *had* to be bad, she thought, but what the hell, she'd let him tell her all about it — dead cats resurrected as monsters, dead children — and then she'd tell him for the nth time that if he really liked horror, he should try Sophocles.

A woman who had just told Danielle her name, though Danielle had already forgotten it, asked how she felt about the possibility of being a senator's wife, would she continue teaching, and a chill went through Danielle even though it was much too hot in the room. She finished her wine, and when a server walked past with a tray, she took another glass. "Well," she said to this woman, "the only way I'll know what it's like to be a senator's wife would be for David to win, so we have to do everything we can to make sure he does."

God, she thought, when I tell David later, he'll laugh at *that* line. They hadn't had time to laugh lately, hadn't seen each other nearly enough. Two more weeks, she told herself as she drank her wine quickly, and back to normal: Sunday brunch, pancakes and scrambled eggs, reading the paper, a drive to Valley Forge, a long hike or a bike ride.

She did have to speak. Not a speech, nothing scripted, but she had to say something. The wine would help. She was comfortable speaking to her college students about plays, but speaking at a political fundraiser was a challenge. Her goal, in practical and slightly crass terms, was to convince people, without directly asking them, to open their wallets. Maybe the money wouldn't help as much now, two weeks from Election Day, as it might have two months earlier. But she had to try — for David.

She realized, as the hostess clinked a wineglass with a butter knife to hush the room, that this might be the last fundraiser she would ever attend, and therefore she wanted to say something new. In the class-room, she spoke with authenticity about what she loved, and there was no reason in this setting to do otherwise.

"Thank you for welcoming us into your home," she said. "David is truly sorry not to be here, but he seems to think that I'm better at this than he is. I can tell you in all honesty that I'm not. Maybe my son Nick is — he's the handsome young man over there in the blue blazer, the one who needs a haircut." Some laughter as everyone turned to look at Nick. "I promised myself that I would be brief, and I intend to keep that promise. We all know how much this election means, and I think we all trust that David would be a devoted senator, that he would represent all of us with as much energy and determination as he's repre-sented so many people over the years — people who were suffering and looking for hope. I want to make sure you know this about David: his practice as a lawyer has not been about personal success or financial gain. Those things have happened, but they're by-products — I know this — of a deeper desire to help people during difficult times, when they're dealing with grief or serious injury."

Danielle paused, and the only sound in the room was the crackling in the fireplaces. "I'm thinking of one girl, seven years old, a beautiful child, who was critically injured in an accident. I think of her often. A station wagon crashed at high speed into the side of the car the girl's father was driving. During the trial, David proved that the brakes in the station wagon were faulty, and the family received financial restitution. They were going to need those resources, and more, as their daughter recovered. She's had more than a dozen surgeries since then, and has learned to walk again, and recently started high school. But here is what I really want to tell you. One night a few months ago, I heard David on the phone. He was in his office at home, and the door was closed. There was something different about his voice, something softer, and, to be honest, I wondered who was on the other end of that call."

A few people chuckled. "When he came out of his office, he had this guilty look on his face," Danielle said, "and now I was *very* curious. But then he told me he'd been speaking to that girl, and to her parents. And that he calls them every year on her birthday. And let me tell you, she's not the only one he calls. He has a Rolodex, separate

16

from the one he uses for work, with the names, numbers, and birthdays of dozens of people he got to know — and care about — by representing them, fighting for them. He never told me, or anyone, that he does this. He didn't want me to know. And I'm sure he wouldn't want me to be telling you. He doesn't do things like that for personal gain or political reasons. Remember, he ran because he was asked to — many times, I should add — by people who believed he would serve the Commonwealth of Pennsylvania with dignity and strength. And I believe that too. And I hope you all do as well, and will support David in whatever ways you can down the homestretch. Thank you again."

Well, her students had never applauded like this. That was one perk of giving such a speech, and she had to admit, it felt good — especially when she looked across the room at Nick clapping proudly. It felt all the better because she meant what she had said. She celebrated with another glass of wine.

An hour later, as they were leaving, Nick said, "Can I drive?"

"Not at night."

"What good is my permit if you guys don't let me drive?"

"Even your father says not at night."

They got into the car, and Danielle started the engine.

But before she drove away, Nick said, "Mom, let's take a walk."

"I'm not drunk."

"I never said you were."

"I'm fine," she said, even though she had drunk her wine quickly — three or four glasses, she couldn't remember — and hadn't eaten anything for fear of getting food stuck in her teeth.

Nick said, "This property is huge, and look at those hedges, they remind me of this scene from *The Shining.*"

"No Stephen King tonight, okay?"

"Snob."

"Absolutely."

"It's almost Halloween, it's foggy, let's just walk around."

"I told you, I'm fine."

"Forget that," Nick said. "I just don't want to go home yet."

Maybe it was Nick's smile — he *was* charming — or maybe she really was tipsy, but suddenly she didn't want to go home yet either. The campaign would be over soon, and she did enjoy some of this, especially the quieter moments when she caught David's eye and just from a glance they exchanged an unspoken inside joke about the absurdity of political campaigns. David's raised eyebrows said, *All this bullshit,* and her smile said, *Are we really doing this?* and his said, *As long as we do it together.* Something about those moments, a shared secret with David, made her feel girlish. When they were seniors at the University of Pennsylvania and she still wasn't sure about David — how could he have dropped Modern Drama for History of the Supreme Court! — he had convinced her to sleep in a sleeping bag with him on the fifty-yard line of Franklin Field as a light December snow covered the grass around them.

Danielle felt that younger woman in her now, and remembered that feeling of being in the sleeping bag with David.

She turned off the car.

They walked along a narrow dirt path bordered by tall hedges cut into the faces of the Founding Fathers. "Now *those* should be in a Stephen King novel," Danielle said, and Nick agreed. As they walked through an apple orchard, Danielle picked an apple and handed it to Nick. He wiped it on his pants as if about to eat it, but then threw it as high and as far as he could. The apple disappeared in the fog. Beyond the orchard was a formal garden, a small pond at its center, and past the garden, under lights, was a clay tennis court. Nick asked Danielle if she wanted to hit a little, and she said sure. Nick stood on one side of the net, his tie loosened, Danielle on the other side. Nick mimed a serve, Danielle moved to her right and mimed a forehand return. They went back and forth like that, an epic rally with Nick doing play-by-play: "Christie with a powerful backhand, but Glass gets to it and somehow smashes an incredible winner that just catches the back line!" Nick dove for the invisible ball and then lay on the court, limbs spread, spent. It had been too long, Danielle thought, since she'd laughed like this, and years since someone had used her maiden name, Glass. Nick stood and jogged to the net to congratulate Danielle on her victory. She brushed the clay off the back of his jacket and said, "Okay, let's head home."

Betsy woke from a dream she couldn't remember except that it must have been pleasant, because she felt safe and her body was heavy in a good way, lying within the outline it made on the mattress. She lay peacefully still in that perfect time just after waking and just before falling back asleep. The phone was ringing. She heard her father get out of bed and walk past her room, and then his voice, quiet: "No. No. No."

When she heard him hang up, Betsy came out of her room. Her father stood by the hallway phone, eyes closed, wearing boxer shorts, a white undershirt, black dress socks. His hair was rumpled. He looked like a boy dressed as a man, like that boyhood photo of Nick wearing their father's undershirt. She asked what was wrong, but her father didn't answer, he just hugged her, too long, and she started to cry even though she didn't yet know about what.

When he told her, she didn't believe him. He said *gone,* which left open the possibility of return.

Let it be Christmas Eve, Betsy thought as her father drove them to the hospital. Midnight Mass was the only reason she'd ever been up at this time, and if it were Christmas Eve then all this could be normal. But she was wearing slippers and a jacket over her nightgown. And it was October, not December. Chilly, not cold. No wreaths on doors, or blinking trees, but pumpkins on porches, ghosts and witches hanging from branches.

Her mother, with her bruised and bandaged face, her swollen lips, could have

21

been wearing a mask. She was asleep, but the nurse used the word *unconscious* — a more frightening word, especially to a ten-year-old. As they stood beside her mother's bed, Betsy thought: We know, but she doesn't. She imagined her mother changing places with Nick. Her mother had lived almost three times as long. She loved her mother, of course she did, but it didn't seem fair that Nick should be the one.

Her mother didn't wake. A man whose job it was to do things just like this, delicate things, took them to see Nick. The man was short and slim and had blue eyes and thinning gray hair. He wore a white shirt and a blue striped tie. Betsy thought it would be a nice tie for her father. They followed him into an elevator, which took them down a little too quickly and gave Betsy a sick feeling in her stomach.

The elevator came to rest, and the doors opened. Her father told her that she didn't have to see. It was the last thing she wanted, but she had to, otherwise she wouldn't believe. Her father said that he was going in first, and Betsy should wait. But she didn't want to be anywhere without him; she insisted on going in. The man led them into a small room, the viewing room, and there beneath a white sheet on a stainless-steel table was the shape of someone she still didn't believe could be Nick.

Her father stood beside the body, and Betsy stood behind him. Then he pulled down the sheet.

He blinked a lot, covered his mouth with his hand, closed his eyes.

Then Betsy looked.

There was a scratch on one side of Nick's face and a trace of blood by his mouth, but otherwise he looked alive. Only a few hours ago he was. He looked as if at any moment he might sit up and say, "Gotcha!" His neck was arched back, his hair mussed, his eyes closed, mouth slightly open. Her father touched Nick's hair, the scratch, his eyelids, and then Betsy did the same, in the same order, as if it were some ritual that would bring him back. Her father took off his sweater, rolled it, and put it beneath Nick's neck to prop up his head.

"You'll see him again," her father said. Betsy wasn't sure whether he meant she'd see the body at the wake or that she'd see her brother in some afterlife she was already trying to imagine.

That night, on a cot in her mother's hospital room, Betsy tried to sleep, but whenever she closed her eyes, Nick hovered above her, breathing white light against her eyelids. And every time she opened her eyes, he wasn't there, the light was gone.

OCTOBER 31, 1984

She didn't have to go, her mother said, but Betsy wanted to. Such a strange feeling as she walked the three blocks to school: Nick was watching her. They had buried him the day before, she had placed a red rose on the casket, suspended over the hole, and yet she felt him now as if he were floating above her. She stopped around the corner from school and stared up at an almost cloudless sky: way up a bird glided across her field of vision. But as soon as she turned the corner and saw her school and a few of her class-mates — they waved to her, then quickly looked away — as soon as she encountered this ordinariness, whatever presence of Nick she'd felt was gone. She wondered if her mother had been right: she should not have come to school, not today.

The youngest children were not in uniform; they were witches and nurses and

Care Bears; there was a Yoda, a Superman, a President Reagan. Betsy wore her uniform — plaid skirt, white blouse, burgundy sweater — so why then did she feel that she too was in costume? There had been a photo in that morning's paper — Betsy holding her father's hand as they left the funeral, her mother behind them, eyes cast down, the bruises on her face visible, a square white bandage over the stitches at her temple — and Betsy felt that in the photo she did not appear to be herself. It was perhaps the only photo of her about which she could say — though she would never actually say this — that she looked pretty. With her brown hair pulled back from her face and with the light makeup she had been permitted to wear, she seemed older — a teenager rather than a ten-year-old girl. She resembled her mother, she thought, her mother as she'd seen her in old photographs. Her mother, however, did not look like herself. Betsy had asked if they could put on their makeup together, but her mother had replied tonelessly and without looking at Betsy that she didn't want any makeup. This made Betsy wonder if she too shouldn't wear any, if there was something inappropriate about light blush and barely noticeable lip gloss on the day of your

26

brother's funeral. She felt guilty for whatever her mother was feeling; she listened for her every word and watched her every expression closely and observed her father doing the same. Just before leaving for the church, her mother checked her bandage in a mirror just as Betsy had checked her hair and her father had checked his tie.

And so as Betsy walked into her classroom, she imagined that she was still in the costume she'd worn the day before — that it was permanent. Her brother's death had made her older and prettier, and she knew things none of her classmates knew.

Her teacher, Mrs. Murrow, hugged her in front of the class, and she felt a thrill knowing that everyone's eyes were on her.

But almost immediately after that, the day settled into its routine. It was Wednesday. If not for the construction paper pumpkins and bats bordering the blackboard, she might have forgotten that it was Halloween. It's Wednesday, she thought over and over, but she'd never understood why it wasn't pronounced Wed-*nes*-day. She and her friends liked to pronounce words phonetically, the way they seemed meant to be pronounced: Feb-*ru*-ary, dic-*tio*-nary. They pronounced silent letters: the *k* in *knight,* the *p* in *psalm,* the *ea* in *beautiful.* Just a

27

silly thing they did to let others know that they were friends. It was just another Wed-*nes*-day — except it wasn't, because all morning she kept catching — *cat*-ching — her classmates looking at her, and others would not look at her, and while they were taking a math quiz — one from which Betsy was exempt but which she insisted on taking — Mrs. Murrow laid her hand on Betsy's back and asked if she was okay, and perhaps this question itself caused her not to be, or caused her to realize that she was not, and she put down her pencil and said, "I've finished my quiz. May I please go home now?"

When her mother arrived to pick her up, Betsy was ashamed of the bruises, the bandage, the stitches, as if *she* were responsible for them. She rushed her mother outside before her friends could see.

"I didn't think you should go to school today," her mother said.

"I wanted to try," Betsy said.

As they walked home, Betsy noticed her mother worrying the bandage; she couldn't tell if her mother was trying to get her fingernail under the adhesive border to peel it off or was making sure it was properly fastened.

■ ■ ■ ■

It was much too big for her, Nick's red football jersey, but Betsy liked having it on. She was slightly chunky — she'd heard her mother use that word to describe her — and it was nice to wear something that made her feel small. She used to feel small too whenever Nick hugged her or lifted her up. He used to sneak up on her from behind and squeeze her love handles, and she would cry out, startled, but then laugh. She didn't like the phrase *love handles. Love* was fine, but *handles* made them seem more than what they were, which were curves, really, a little extra flesh around her waist. Beneath Nick's jersey, which reached her knees, she had no curves that anyone could see.

She lay curled up in bed, facing the window, waiting for night to darken her unlit room. On her nightstand she kept a black shortwave radio — a tenth-birthday gift from Nick. She'd asked for one because she was proficient in Spanish and had even started learning German. But what she'd ended up liking even more about the radio was that it kept her company at night and helped her fall asleep, especially when she listened to languages she didn't know. She reached for it now and brought it into bed with her. Even the click it made when turned on she found comforting, and its red on-light, and her careful rotation of its round tuning dial, and the wonderful moment when a human voice from the other side of the world found its way across a sea of static to her ears.

For a few minutes she listened to a Japanese woman who spoke with a girl-high pitch and soothing inflection. She wasn't reading the news — there were too many long pauses and too much sympathy in her voice, that was what it sounded like to Betsy, a sincere offering of condolences — and Betsy wanted to know what the woman was actually saying.

The doorbell rang. Betsy must have fallen asleep. The Japanese woman was gone, replaced by a Japanese man who spoke too fast and sounded belligerent; she imagined the man speaking too close to her, gesticulating wildly. She turned the dial a few degrees until faintly, through static, she heard a boy's voice. She sat up suddenly and pressed the radio to her ear. The boy was speaking English, she was pretty sure. His voice must have recently changed; it broke, then deepened again. She couldn't make out any words. Then he faded away. The bell rang again, and again, and so she got up to answer the door.

When she reached the top of the stairs, she saw her mother sitting on the bottom step, her back to Betsy. She was a few feet from the front door but made no move to answer it. Betsy walked down the stairs toward her mother. She could hear the voices of children on the other side of the door; she imagined them in costumes, holding bags filled with candy. "The porch light is on," she heard a woman say.

It was unlike Betsy, this gesture, but there was something about the curve of her mother's spine, how she sat slouched on the bottom step wearing a thin white cardigan. Betsy sat behind her mother and wrapped her arms around her.

Her mother jumped up as if she'd seen a ghost. Betsy was frightened now too — and confused.

"Take that off."

Betsy didn't understand.

And then she did, and she started to cry.

Her father must have heard; he came to the stairs, his hair mussed as if he too had been sleeping. It was only seven o'clock.

"Who was at the door?" he said.

"I'm sorry," Betsy said through tears.

"What happened?" her father said.

"I need her to take that off," her mother said.

"I didn't mean anything."

"Of course not," her father said.

The bell rang again. Her father looked through the eyehole and then turned off the porch light. He took her mother into the living room. Betsy stayed where she was and listened to them whisper.

"The jersey, the sleeves when she hugged me, it frightened me."

"It's okay now."

"No, it's not."

"She lost her brother."

"I can't look at that jersey."

"Okay."

"I'm sorry, I just can't."

"Okay, but lower your voice."

"Betsy," her mother called, "stop listening and go upstairs."

"Lower your voice, please," her father said.

Betsy went back to her room. She wouldn't take it off, she decided. As long as her mother didn't have to see it — that was all that mattered. She kneeled by her window and looked out at the trick-or-treaters walking past her darkened house to the next porch, which was lit, and more children came and walked past, and more, and then fewer, and soon Delancey Place was quiet.

In the middle of the night, David heard her crying. He got out of bed, careful not to wake Danielle, and went to her room. She was whimpering in her sleep; he hadn't heard her do that in years. He waited for it to stop, and when it didn't, he turned down her covers, lifted her, and carried her to his room. She was still wearing Nick's jersey, and he considered pulling it over her head but decided that was unnecessary. He laid her in the middle of the bed, beside Danielle, and then he got in and pulled up the covers. Neither Betsy nor Danielle had woken. But now he was wide awake, and as peaceful as it felt to have Betsy in bed beside him, maybe even because of how nice it felt, the agony of yesterday — the casket lowered into the hole, eventually having to walk away, to go home — returned to him, and there was nothing to do except clench and unclench his fists under the covers and listen to his daughter's breathing.

Three hours later, in darkness, Danielle gone from bed, David woke with his fists still clenched, his fingers sore.

NOVEMBER 2, 1984

David knew there was a fine line between sincerity and show. Actually, he thought, they often overlapped. He'd had to negotiate the relationship between the two during the campaign and, before that, as a trial lawyer. Both jobs required sincerity as well as exaggeration. How things were and how others perceived them. Genuine emotions and manufactured emotions. Most of his clients had been injured in car accidents, many caused by drunk driving, injuries ranging from whiplash to paralysis. Some clients were the families of those killed, survivors suing for damages. As an attorney, he understood how to put a number on such loss, some figure the family tried to believe could compensate for even a fraction of their pain. It was never enough, but there *was* a number. When he spoke about a family's grief, he did feel it — not exactly what they felt, but something — and he never doubted that the work he did on behalf of his clients was valuable. He believed that he was good at what he did at least in part because he could sufficiently imagine the pain of a man who would never walk again or have sex with his wife again, or the sorrow of a mother who'd had to bury her child. He felt for them and channeled his emotions into his work, even before the accident that took Nick. But now he knew that there really was no number.

David thought about sincerity and show, real emotions and manufactured ones, as he stood beside Betsy on the sideline of Nick's high school football field, only a few miles from where the accident had taken place. It was Friday night, four days before the election.

Danielle had not come; she couldn't, she said.

The team had retired Nick's number ten and planned to keep his locker as it was: his helmet, his cleats, his white home jersey hanging from a hook. When the coach showed David and Betsy the locker — the team was already on the field, warming up — David noticed on a shelf behind the jersey a bottle of shampoo and a spray can of deodorant, and while he could imagine the jersey and helmet and cleats in the locker forever, he did not want to return here years from now and see the deodorant and shampoo bottle, its cap missing. Without asking the coach if it was all right, David removed the shampoo and deodorant and put them in the trash.

David put his hand over his heart as the national anthem played through the stadium's speakers, and when the song ended, he expected the announcer to ask for a moment of silence.

But the teams took the field and the visiting team kicked off and the kick returner on Nick's team — David still thought of the team as Nick's — ran the ball out to the thirty-yard line. The offense ran onto the field, and David was confused. Why were he and Betsy standing there on the sideline? Were they expected to watch the entire game? And then he noticed that while the players on both teams were in their positions, the linemen in their stances, ready for the snap, no one stood behind center. No player moved. The stadium was silent. Thirty seconds passed, a minute, the silence went on — and yes, David thought, such gestures mattered. And this kind of silence, rather than the kind he had expected, allowed him to see Nick's physical absence, to feel it, in a way he might not have otherwise. There was no quarterback.

The referee blew his whistle and the center stood and ran the ball to the sideline and gave it to David. Then he gave Betsy Nick's captain's armband. David shook the boy's hand, and then the game resumed with a new starting quarterback.

NOVEMBER 6, 1984

David voted early in the morning but wanted nothing to do with election night. So he made a plan. He'd arranged things with Penn Public Safety. He and Danielle were alums, after all, and he *was* running for the Senate, at least for a few more hours. An officer met him in the parking lot, walked him to the stadium, and unlocked the gate. David led Danielle and Betsy to the fifty-yard line of Franklin Field, where he unrolled a queen-size sleeping bag and laid a blanket beside it on the cold grass. He'd made peanut butter and jelly sandwiches and brought a thermos of hot tea, and they sat on the blanket and ate dinner while David told Betsy — he'd told her many times before — the story of how he and Danielle had snuck onto this same field twenty-five years earlier and slept in a sleeping bag, and how people used to say that

38

Danielle looked like Jackie O, and how David had to woo Danielle because he'd dropped Modern Drama, and Danielle finally added a few details ("I liked your father, he had nice hair and a great smile, but I just wasn't sure about him"), and David could see that Betsy enjoyed hearing this story again.

David checked his pocket not for the first time, feeling for his concession speech, which he'd folded into a square the size of the bandage on Danielle's face. The bandage, he noticed, had come loose on two sides and looked about to fall off. Normally he might have reached over and pressed it back on, but nothing was normal, he remembered, and he was afraid to touch Danielle.

He was surprised when Betsy did. But rather than reaffix it, she ripped it off, exposing the stitches. Danielle said nothing. She didn't scold Betsy, as David expected her to. Her eyes filled, but she blinked back the tears. She touched the wound, running her hand along the stitches.

It started to snow lightly, and the tea was gone, and Betsy said her hands were cold, and so they all got into the sleeping bag, Betsy in the middle. It was a tight fit for three, but warm. Danielle lay with her arms at her sides. They let snow fall on their faces, Betsy opening her mouth to taste it. David was glad to be here as the polls closed, the field now coated with the thinnest blanket of snow. He reached for Danielle's hand and held it, and felt no pressure in return, but he would not let go no matter if she never returned his gesture.

But then he felt her hand squeeze his. He wrapped his arm around Betsy, and Danielle did the same, and he thought: For now, this is enough. We are here. We are still here. Our daughter is. She needs us.

When they got home, an hour after the polls had closed, the phone was ringing. It was Mike Bennett, David's campaign manager.

"Where have you been?"

"I told you."

"You said you'd be home *before* the polls closed."

"We fell asleep."

"You have a speech to give."

"I decided I'm going to call Groff to congratulate him, and that's that. Who came up with the idea for a concession speech anyway? Hold on," David said. He laid the phone's receiver on the kitchen counter, took the square of paper out of his pocket, unfolded it, held it near the receiver, and

40

tore it into pieces. He picked up the phone. "Did you hear that? That was my concession speech."

"You don't need to give one."

"What do you mean?"

"Congratulations, David."

"I don't believe you."

"Senator David Christie," Mike said. "How does that sound?"

"It sounds — I don't know," David said.

"It sounds great," Mike said.

"How close was it?"

"As close as it gets."

"I can't *believe* it."

"Things turned the past two weeks."

After a pause, during which David couldn't think of what to say, Mike said, "A car will pick you up in twenty minutes."

When David hung up the phone, he walked down the hallway toward his room. He stopped outside Betsy's room; he heard a German man's voice coming from inside — her shortwave radio, he realized. His bedroom door was closed too. He could hear Danielle opening and closing drawers, probably getting changed for bed. She had been going to bed hours earlier than usual and waking when it was still dark. He wasn't sure how to tell her what had happened or how it had happened — sympathy votes, he

41

assumed. He would have to ask her to put on a dress, and to help Betsy put one on, and tell them that a car would be here soon to take them down to Old City, where he would say what? There wasn't anything he wanted to talk about other than Nick. And his family. Why couldn't he simply do that? Congratulate Senator Groff on his twelve years of service in the Senate and a well-run campaign, thank his staff, speak honestly about the past two weeks, and reassure Pennsylvanians that come January he would be ready — he did not know if this was true — to serve their interests in Washington. A short speech. No sentimental clichés about winning this for Nick. Just the truth: that he missed his son, and that this was bittersweet.

He wasn't ready to walk into the bedroom; he wasn't ready to tell Danielle, or anyone. He felt a wave of heat on his face, but when he touched his forehead, it was cold and clammy. He went into the bathroom and splashed his face with cold water. Light-headed, he cupped his hands together and let them fill with water. As he drank from his hands, he started to feel better, but when he raised his head, he felt much worse. He hurried to the toilet, kneeled on the floor, and got sick.

DECEMBER 6, 1984

At Buchanan College, an hour west of Philadelphia, Danielle walked into the classroom prepared to give her final lecture of the semester. She was afraid to give it, and so she had practiced: how *tragedy* is a slippery word made more so by every new theory about it; how if you try to define tragedy, someone very smart will find an exception; how tragedy in reference to art and tragedy in reference to life are not the same; how too often the word is used as a replacement for *sad;* how tragedy must involve suffering but all suffering isn't necessarily tragic; how the so-called tragedies they had read that semester, by the beauty of the words used to create them — the slightest form of redemption — might not be tragedies after all; how perhaps true tragedies are not turned into art but are suffered in private.

She laid her notes on the desk and looked at her students staring at her. They were only a few years older than her son would ever be. One student, Cal Westfall, a freshman but the best student in the class, raised his hand.

Before she could call on Cal, she had a panic attack.

By the time she reached the ladies' room, she was having trouble breathing. She locked herself in a stall, where she sat on the toilet seat. She finger-pressed one of her nostrils closed and tried to breathe slowly.

A few minutes later, she heard the bathroom door open, then the voices of two students from her class. One of the girls went into the next stall. Danielle, afraid the other girl would recognize her shoes, lifted her feet. The girl, upon glancing beneath the door and believing the stall to be empty, tried to push open the door. She kept pushing, harder, and Danielle said, "There's someone in here," and the girl said, "Sorry."

Danielle felt that she might die, and that to die wouldn't be so terrible, and with this thought some of her anxiety lifted — enough for her to walk back to class, ten minutes late.

She stood outside the room, staring at her empty chair, her notes on the desk, before walking in. Everyone stopped talking and looked at her.

"I'm sorry," she said, "but I'm not feeling well. I'm going to hold office hours instead of class — in case you have questions about the final."

She gathered her notes, but before she could leave, Cal said, "Professor, we got you something." He walked to the front of the class and handed her a gift. Even though it was wrapped, she could tell by its shape and weight that it was a book. She hadn't expected this at all. She knew that the gesture wasn't just because this was the last class, but that it also had to do with the accident. The class had gone through it with her, in a way. They'd been mature. They'd known how to offer condolences like adults. They'd said, "I was so sorry to hear, Professor," or some version of that, before moving on to the business of class.

She stood there holding their gift and thought, I should have gotten *them* a gift. She was afraid she might cry. Had she tried to speak, even to say thank you, she wouldn't have been able. She wanted to open the gift later, in her office, but they were all looking at her. It was obvious that they wanted her to open it.

She peeled off the wrapping paper slowly,

and this helped focus her and calm her nerves. She couldn't believe what it was — it was too expensive, it couldn't be, but it was, the pink dust jacket, the haunting Alvin Lustig drawing, *A Streetcar Named Desire,* 1947 first edition. They knew it was her favorite.

"This is too much," she said.

"If it makes you feel better," Cal said, "my aunt owns an antiquarian bookstore, so we got a family discount."

"That makes me feel a *little* better," she said. "I'll cherish this. Thank you all very much."

In her office she had a bottle of red wine left over from an evening department meeting a week earlier — the first meeting she had attended since the accident; it took all of her strength and composure to get through her classes. Now, she poured wine into a coffee mug; she stared down into the wine before taking a sip. Her office hours had begun, but she couldn't bring herself to open the door.

She opened *Streetcar* and lifted it to her face. The smell reminded her of other old books she had smelled and the places she had smelled them — used-book stores in New York and London — and the quiet, peaceful feeling she associated with such places. Sometimes, when she was daydreaming before class, the memory of a specific bookstore, maybe one in Boston or Los Angeles she'd been to only once, would pop into her head in great detail — the storefront, the lighting, the layout of the shelves, the register, the face of the person behind the counter, the books she'd bought.

She heard voices outside her door — a young man and woman from her class. There was a knock, but she didn't move.

After they were gone, she drank the wine she'd poured. She poured some more and drank it quickly, then lay on the couch in her office and closed her eyes.

SPRING 1985

The first time Betsy heard her mother say into the phone to her father, "Remember, tomorrow is a good day to try," she registered it as curious — try what? — but not curious enough that Betsy thought *too* much about it. But when her mother said the same thing a month later, leaning against the kitchen counter, the phone receiver cradled between her shoulder and face so that she could peel an apple for Betsy, she knew that whatever *to try* meant, she wasn't supposed to know.

One day after school, she went into Nick's room. She went in there at least once every day, sometimes just to lie on his bed, which made her feel closer to him, and look across the room at his clothes still hanging in his closet. She didn't expect to find her mother sitting on Nick's bed, blouse unbuttoned, head down, deep in concentration, pushing a needle into the flesh of her stomach, pinched between her fingers.

Betsy froze in the doorway, unable to continue into the room or back out. Her mother looked up, startled, and dropped the needle. Betsy thought she'd caused her mother to prick herself. Her mother said, "Betsy, how many times have I told you to knock on any closed door."

Betsy said that she was sorry and went to her room.

She didn't understand why they wanted another when they already had one. When they'd had two, there had been no desire for three, but now that they had one, they wanted two again. She was pretty sure it was her mother who wanted another and her father who wanted whatever her mother wanted, whatever might make her *her* again.

Her father was in DC during the week, her mother was teaching at Buchanan College on Tuesdays and Thursdays, and Betsy was in fifth grade, trying to be more like Nick. She was no athlete, like her brother had been, but she had joined cross-country. She couldn't throw or catch or shoot or dribble or kick a ball, any kind of ball, not well, but she could run.

She ran with her father on weekends. She

tried to keep up but couldn't, even though he ran more slowly than he would have alone or with Nick. Too soon she'd have to walk, a terrible cramp in her side, her lungs burning, and her father would stop and walk with her. He was kind that way; he encouraged her. But she was doing this more for her mother. If she wanted to impress her father, it was so that he would report back to her mother what a good runner she was, or at least how hard she'd tried, and maybe then her mother wouldn't want another, maybe she'd be fine with just Betsy.

And so one Saturday morning that first spring without Nick, Betsy pushed herself past the cramp in her side and the burning in her lungs and into the nausea that comes after. Her father had coached her to push through discomfort but to listen to her body, two pieces of advice that seemed at odds. She ran off the path and out of sight to the edge of the river they'd been running alongside and got sick, and she thought: Mom will hear about this and not want another. She will remember that she already has a child who gets sick and needs help and is here and alive but has been feeling invisible, a living, breathing ghost.

They walked home along the river and then through the city, and her father put his arm around her and made sure they stopped for water and pressed the water fountain button for her. She was dizzy and felt warm despite the cool spring morning, but the longer they walked, the cooler she became, and the sweat on her face and back grew cold.

When they arrived home and her mother asked how she did, her father said, "We had a nice run. It's beautiful out." Even though he was being kind by not telling her mother that Betsy had gotten sick, Betsy wanted her to know. "It was harder than I thought," she said, hoping her father would say the rest, that she'd tried hard but gotten sick, but he didn't. "I feel a little woozy," she said, again hoping her father would take her cue, but he brought Betsy a glass of water and kissed her forehead. Finally she said, "I got sick," but her mother didn't hear. She was sitting cross-legged on the couch with a book on her lap, some tragedy she must have been teaching that week. Betsy could see the dog-eared pages and the passages her mother had underlined and her notes in the margins, but she could tell that her mother wasn't reading. Her hands held the book open on her lap, but she was staring across the room at nothing.

■ ■ ■ ■

PART TWO:
KISS AND TELL

2010

■ ■ ■ ■

FEBRUARY 14, 2010

She bikes the two miles conscious of her ass.

Not whether it looks good, or whether biking will make it look good, but what her ass might be doing to the photo in the back pocket of her jeans: a handsome man holding a baby, both of them blurred.

It's just a color copy of a photo from a tabloid, almost as old as she is, but she doesn't want it to be *too* creased. She stops at the side of the road, moves the photo to her coat pocket, then continues biking.

She has a folder on her computer, deeply buried and password-protected: tabloid pieces, embarrassing photos, articles from legit papers too. Downloads of books. Reviews, customer comments. So many books, so many contradictions; with every new word written the truth becomes murkier.

She's read, as far as she knows, everything written about this family. Seventeen years old, a second-semester college student, and already she has a PhD in *them.* Had David written a memoir, she could read it to him, a note from him then to him now. She could remind him of who he was and what he did. She could show him the photo in her pocket. But memoirs aren't true, she thinks. A memoirist always has an eye on history; a memoirist spins the truth the way a politician does; a memoirist confesses and confesses but never to the worst; a memoirist reveals all his secrets but the darkest. One biography claims that *To Kill a Mockingbird* was David's favorite book and made him want to be a lawyer; another claims that his favorite was *All the King's Men,* which seems such the obvious choice, Avery thinks as she bikes the final bitch of a hill, that it *must* be made up.

She tells the gray-haired woman at the front desk of the nursing care facility that she is here to see David Christie. "I'm a relative of his," she says. She explains that this is the first time she's been able to come see him and then asks the woman what room David is in. The woman tells Avery the room number and asks her to sign in. Avery writes her real name, then realizes, as she walks down the long hallway to his room, that it isn't *really* her name. Not the name she was born with. She had to wait until she was sixteen to change it. She'd been a hyphen but didn't want her mother's or father's name anymore. So she made up a new one: Avery Modern. She just liked the sound of it. Newness. Now. A break from the past.

Her mother was hurt. Not because she wanted Avery to keep *her* name but because she wanted Avery to keep her father's name.

Even with a new name, finally away at Buchanan College — a choice that hurt her mother even more than Avery's new name — she's still afraid someone will know who she really is. Her childhood home was often dark, the blinds drawn. Some days, after months of nothing, the bell would ring, a camera would flash, and her mother would slam the door.

The door to his room is ajar. She knocks, but when no one says "come in," she pushes the door open anyway. It's a large room divided into three areas. On the far side, by the window, are a bed and dresser. The side of the room closest to the door is a living area with a love seat, two chairs, and a TV mounted on the wall. Between the living area and the bed are a desk and a small bookcase.

Avery walks in to get a closer look at the framed photo on the dresser: a younger David, his wife, their two children. She looks at their faces, into their eyes, the photo taken years before she, Avery, was born, and then she hears faintly a man's voice, "I'm sorry," and a woman's voice, "It's okay, it's okay." She was so fixated on the photo that she didn't notice until now the open bathroom door: he is sitting on the toilet, a nurse cleaning him, a wheelchair beside the toilet. She goes back into the hallway to wait.

She has thought about this moment for months, ever since she discovered online that David had moved into this facility. She has prepared for it as much as one can prepare for something like this. She has the photo and plans to show it to him. Maybe that's the first thing she should do. But what she didn't consider, she realizes as the nurse opens the door and sees her, is what to say if asked in front of him who she is. She could say exactly what she wrote when she signed in: her name. Maybe just her first name, leave it at that. She could say "just a friend." She could lie, not a great idea, and say she's a volunteer who visits people who don't get many visitors.

But before the nurse can say anything, David recognizes her. Or seems to.

"Hello," he whispers. "It's nice to see you again."

Avery can barely hear him. The nurse explains that he speaks only in whispers now. "Sometimes you have to lean in close," she says.

"She knows," he says.

Then to Avery: "It's been a while."

She walks over to him and stands beside his chair. She tries not to betray her shock. She already knew from photos of him online that his hair is gray, but his body shaking this much, especially his hands — no photo could ever show that.

He was every bit as good as Clinton at making people believe him. Clinton bit his lip and squinted to seem sincere, whereas David did this thing with his jaw, he would flex it, the bones would kind of pop. It seemed involuntary, and maybe that was its power. It gave the impression of simultaneous stillness and motion, vulnerability and strength. He never used any of those cliché politician hand gestures like the Clinton thumb, which was really the Kennedy thumb, fist closed, thumb resting against the thumbside of the index finger and slightly extended, a way of pointing without pointing; or the hand steeple, where the fingers come together to form a little rooftop. Not David Christie; he kept his fingers interlocked as if in prayer, or palms down on a dais, arms slightly tensed, torso leaning forward. Early in his career he used to keep his hands in his pockets. Someone smart must have told him not to; looks like you're hiding something. Maybe the jaw flex is something not everyone can do, like rolling your tongue. No doubt someone on his campaign noticed it and said, "Keep doing that thing with your jaw, it plays well," and maybe David said, "What thing with my jaw?"

Avery has looked in a mirror and tried, but all that happens is she grinds her teeth or moves her lips into a pout or twitches her nose or furrows her brows. She ends up looking menacing or ridiculous or both. David must not be aware of it, because he still does it — right now, in fact. Even as the Parkinson's causes him to shake in his wheelchair, a quick flex of his jaw makes him look dignified. He's trim and still dresses sharp: gray slacks, white oxford, brown leather loafers.

"In the closet," he whispers, and at first

Avery thinks he's telling her to get into the closet.

She comes to understand that he's asking her to open the closet. She slides open the door: three suits, a dozen or more button-down shirts, and what must be fifty ties — all of them blue.

"You pick," he says.

As she's looking through the ties, more dark blue than light, he whispers in his chair behind her, "It's nice to see you again."

"You certainly like the color blue," she says, even though she already knew this about him.

She chooses navy with a pattern of alternating thin and thicker white stripes. She's not sure what to do with it.

"I know you know how to tie a tie," he whispers.

"I'm sorry, but I don't."

"I taught you myself."

"I must have forgotten."

She lays the tie on his lap. He manages to pick it up, but his shaking causes him to drop it. She picks it up, brushes it clean with her hand.

"My doctor told me this would happen," he says, "but I was sure I'd figure out a way to cheat it."

"Did I choose the right one?" she says.

"You look good, honey," he says.

That word, *honey*, what a father might say to his daughter.

"Let me get the nurse," she says.

"Betsy, wait," he says, but she leaves.

She walks down the long hallway to the lobby, where old people — older than David — sleep away the day like cats. She stops at the nurses' station and tells the first one she sees that David Christie needs help getting dressed. The nurse smiles and says, "Okay, we'll have someone check on him."

Only when she's outside, about to unlock her bike, does Avery realize that she's still clutching the tie. She takes a few steps back toward the entrance, but stops. She folds the tie and puts it into her coat pocket with the photo. She unlocks her bike and begins the ride back to campus, her face and hands cold against the wind.

Betsy wakes feeling sick. Not like she has the flu, something closer to the blahs, not just a sulky something but a deep fear in her stomach.

"What's wrong?" Cal says.

"Just an upset stomach."

"Are you sure it's nothing else?"

"I'll be fine," she says.

She knows what Cal is thinking — that

this is about her father. As far as he's concerned, everything about Betsy, including any issues in their relationship, can be traced back to her father.

Betsy wants to cancel and almost says something, but they've canceled twice before — *she* has.

An hour later, as they walk to the bakery, she worries about being recognized. Probably silly to worry, but every so often, especially here in Philadelphia, someone will say, "Aren't you . . ." and then try to remember why her face seems familiar, but before the person can finish the question, she will say, "Yes, I am," or, "No, you must be mistaken." It doesn't happen *that* often, but it's something she doesn't want to happen while she's on her way to choose a wedding cake.

By the time they arrive at the bakery, the feeling in her stomach is stronger. In the back, behind a glass partition, under dim lights, a woman wearing a white apron kneads dough. She looks around Betsy's age. She sees them waiting and comes out. "You must be Cal and Betsy," she says. Her name is Sara. She has curly blonde hair and brown eyes and a body similar to Betsy's — extra weight in her belly and hips.

Sara brings out six cupcakes on a tray,

three for each of them. Cal, eight years older than Betsy, is good at delaying gratification. He will go for a long run first thing and have breakfast to look forward to. He will eat his toast before his oatmeal, because he enjoys oatmeal more than toast, and only then will he eat two hard-boiled egg whites, because he likes them best. He nibbles the tip of each egg, and as soon as he reaches the yolk he pops it out onto his plate and finishes the egg white. At the end of breakfast, two perfectly round yolks are all that remain on his otherwise clean plate. Meanwhile, long ago Betsy will have finished her own breakfast — scrambled eggs first because she likes them best, then yogurt because she likes it second best, and finally toast because she likes it the least.

So it makes sense that Cal reaches first for the chocolate cupcake with chocolate icing, his least favorite, while Betsy tries the red velvet with buttercream icing, her favorite. "Happy Valentine's Day," Cal says. He taps his cupcake against Betsy's as if clinking glasses during a toast. They each take a bite. "Hold on," he says. "I can do better than that." He puts down his cupcake, takes Betsy's and sets it on the table, takes her hand, and kisses her engagement ring. "I'm glad we're choosing a cake today," he says, and she smiles and says, "Me too."

Betsy eats the entire cupcake; Cal takes only a few more bites. The yellow cupcake with lemon icing is fine, and the chocolate cupcake with chocolate icing is fine, but Betsy decides on red velvet for the cake. On Cal's plate are three partly eaten cupcakes and on Betsy's plate is nothing.

Sara excuses herself to speak with another customer, and Cal excuses himself to use the restroom. By the time they return to the table, there are two empty plates, not a crumb of cupcake anywhere.

Later, as they walk through the city, Betsy says, "I don't know why I ate so much."

"I think you're beautiful, you know, exactly as you are," Cal says.

She puts her arm around his waist. "Thank you."

"You don't need to thank me for finding you beautiful."

That really stumps Betsy, and after a period of silence Cal says, "I want *you* to think you're beautiful."

And to that Betsy can only think to say, "What's beautiful?"

"Those girls might be the two most beautiful creatures I've ever seen."

Betsy's talking about Cal's nieces, his

sister's twins. She and Cal have taken them to a playground.

Every time Betsy sees them she just wants to stare at them or touch their soft blonde hair or kiss their pouty lips. They are nice children too — well-behaved and polite — and just silly enough. They say the strange-creative-honest-intelligent-charming things precocious children tend to say but adults do not.

If not for the feeling in her stomach and the panic in her chest, Betsy might be able to sit on the park bench watching Cal on the seesaw with the girls and think, That could be us, but instead she thinks: What's wrong with me that I can't look at this man I love and these pouty angels and imagine wanting something like this?

The girls pull Betsy to a rainbow-colored spinning wheel, and Cal spins them so fast that the blah feeling spreads through Betsy's body, to her head and fingers and toes, but not out, and when the wheel stops, the world does not. She tries to stand as still as possible but has to hold the wheel's handle not to fall.

Later, one of the twins — the one with a birthmark on the back of her hand — puts her hand on Betsy's stomach and says, "Do you have a baby in your belly?"

"Just cupcakes."

Betsy's mention of cupcakes triggers a wave of nausea. She goes into the playground's public restroom and stands in a stall and closes her eyes and takes deep breaths.

Then suddenly that old feeling returns, the one she felt after Nick died, where she's lost and needs to get home, except home isn't home, there's nowhere on the planet she can go to end this feeling, and the people she's supposed to know, like Cal, are strangers. Even she's a stranger. She's lost inside her body and needs to get out.

If I could throw up this lost feeling and flush it down the toilet, she thinks, that might be a step in the right direction. But it won't come up, whatever this is, cupcakes but not *really* cupcakes.

So she leaves.

She walks away. Keeps walking. Then runs. Then, when she gets tired and feels sicker, she walks again. She keeps going with no idea *where.* She doesn't look back. She doesn't think anyone saw her go.

On Walnut, a young woman wearing a faux-fur hat asks Betsy if she's decided whom she's voting for. As terrible as she feels, she doesn't want to be rude, so she stops and pretends to listen as the woman tells her about someone running for something and hands her a flyer.

She keeps walking, unsure what she's looking for until she sees it: through a large glass window, a woman with her head inside a hood dryer. Betsy imagines that under the dryer, it is both extremely loud and utterly quiet. A good place, maybe the only place, to hide.

The young man who cuts her hair talks and talks, mostly about himself and his boyfriend and his ex and a Weimaraner named Frisco that belonged to all of them at one time or another but started with the current boyfriend yet somehow ended up with the ex. Betsy can't follow the logic of it, but his voice is a distraction — just as effective, she imagines, as the hood dryer. He talks so much that he never asks one thing about Betsy except what she wants him to do to her hair. She tells him he can do whatever he wants.

She keeps her eyes closed as he cuts. "Don't be scared, honey," the man says.

"I want to be surprised," she says.

Later, when she peeks, her hair is the shortest it's been since she was a girl — bangs in front, to her shoulders in back. She thinks it makes her face look rounder.

The dryer turns out to be just loud, and

makes her internal voice that much louder to compete with it — worries about the wedding, and how many times her phone has vibrated in her pocket, how upset Cal will be, and what she might eat for lunch and dinner to make up for her cupcake gluttony — and there it is again, the feeling in her belly.

She pushes the dryer up off her head and hurries to the restroom, where she kneels over the toilet, and finally it comes up in three great heaves.

Someone knocks on the door and asks if she's okay, and she puts on her best okay voice and says, "I'm fine."

When she emerges from the restroom, her hair still damp, she tells the young man who cut her hair that she's sorry but she has to leave. Her stomach feels better, but the anxiety is now in her chest, and she regrets that she walked away from Cal, didn't answer his calls, worried him — again.

Outside, she closes her eyes, tries to breathe in through her nose, out through her mouth. She's teetering on the edge of the kind of panic attack she started to have last year in New York.

She walks home slowly, occasionally stopping to look in storefront windows, wondering who's staring back at her.

She's not sure how she knows. She's not sure why seeing Cal when she gets home makes her know. But she knows.

And as soon as she knows — she doesn't doubt it for a single beat of her heart — she starts to cry quietly.

"Do you know how much you worried me?" Cal says. He keeps rubbing his hand over his buzz cut, what he does when he's nervous.

"I'm sorry. I'm kind of a mess."

"You're not a mess."

"Please stop saying I'm not when I am."

"You're just going through something," he says.

"I'm sorry I walked away," she says. "I was having one of my things."

"An anxiety attack."

"Yes."

"You could have told me."

"I just needed to be alone."

"So you cut your hair."

"*I* didn't cut it."

"Good," Cal says. "If you did, I'd really be concerned."

"Do I still look like me?"

Gently, with his hand on her chin, he

makes her look at him. "Still you."

She lays her head on his shoulder, and he rubs her back. "Whatever this is," he says, "it's going to be okay."

She wants to tell him that it doesn't *feel* okay, that she's scared, that this feeling has gotten worse since they moved back into the house on Delancey where she grew up, and where her brother didn't grow all the way up, and where her mother died.

She wants to tell him what she now knows, about the baby inside her, but can't say the words.

Avery should call her mother, she really should, but she and Peter Swann are kissing.

It's *so* not her to be doing this, and she would have guessed it was *so* not Peter Swann to be doing this, but people surprise you. Avery saw Peter at the library earlier — she was on her way in, he was on his way out — and when she asked where he was going, he said, "To give out free hugs."

"Why?"

"You don't know about this?"

"Should I?"

"Apparently, it's a Valentine's Day tradition at Buchanan," Peter told her. "It started years ago as a protest against the commercialization of love — something like that."

"I didn't know you were such an activist," Avery said.

"Just for that, you're coming with me."

"I don't think so," Avery said, but Peter took her by the arm and led her out of the library. She made a pretense of resisting.

What Peter didn't mention to Avery was that they'd be giving out hugs *and* kisses. Other students are stationed throughout campus; Avery and Peter are in front of the campus center. Some students they kiss on the cheek, some on the lips, mouths closed — friend kisses. Avery is kissing boys and girls. Peter is kissing girls. The boys he hugs — real hugs, not one-armed dude hugs. A few guys he knows well he gives the European kiss-kiss on both cheeks.

It's freezing, but the hugs and kisses help.

During a lull, Peter turns to Avery and says, "Hey, I have an idea."

But before he says what his idea is, her phone rings.

Even before she looks, she knows who it is.

Her mother — again.

She's called three times since Peter and Avery have been out here. Avery hasn't answered.

Valentine's Day has always been tough on her mother. It's a reminder that she's alone. It's also the day, talk about irony, that started the whole mess.

Actually, the mess began before that.

Avery doesn't answer — again.

My mother, Avery thinks, should be the one here, not me. Her mother would be great at this — giving out hugs and kisses. It's not that she's generous, though she can be, but more that she's kind of needy and love-starved. She'd probably give long hugs, and kiss people in places like their noses and eyes. Not in a creepy way. She'd mean it.

Avery silences her phone and says to Peter, "So what's your big idea?"

Avery knows Peter from a course she's taking called Presidential Politics. This week they've been discussing the role of scandal in presidential elections. All anyone wants to talk about is Bill and Monica — the cigar, the stained blue dress, that stupid Nicholson Baker novel. As if they remember; as if they weren't like five years old. Only Peter Swann, a tall, bookish guy with horn-rimmed glasses, has brought up the human side of the story — Chelsea walking between her parents, holding their hands. Peter says that was right out of the political playbook, but Avery believes it was genuine.

People know about JFK and Marilyn, but Peter Swann knows about Angie Dickinson and Kim Novak and Blaze Starr and Mary Pinchot Meyer. The professor was impressed. Avery, intellectually competitive, brought up Meyer's murder in 1964, less than a year after JFK was assassinated, and how she used to bring marijuana and LSD to the White House. Peter turned and gave her this look, and when class ended he said to her, "Who *are* you?"

They got coffee and had a geek-off about political scandals. It's unlike Avery to do something like that. Number one, she tends not to trust people, especially not boys. Number two, she tends not to talk politics. Not that they were talking politics. For her, it was more like talking literature, or what could make great literature if only people knew the smaller, private details.

Peter knows *too* much, like her. It *has* to be personal, Avery thinks. People know things for a reason. His parents are divorced, one of the first things he told her, but he connected it to politics: "I remember the whole Monica thing because that was right when my parents divorced." Peter knows about Thomas Jefferson and Sally Hemings.

He knows about Grover Cleveland: how he allegedly raped and impregnated a woman named Maria Halpin, had her committed to an asylum, and arranged for the abduction of their child. He knows that Cleveland pretty much raised his future wife — the daughter of his late friend. He knows that Warren Harding had a long affair with Carrie Phillips, a married Germanophile who saved hundreds of his love letters. Her husband, a close friend of Harding's, became an alcoholic and in later years walked the streets of Marion, Ohio, begging for money to buy drinks. Another Harding mistress, Nan Britton, thirty years his junior, had been obsessed with him when she was a girl, covering her bedroom walls with images of him from newspapers and magazines. In 1927 she published the first kiss-and-tell-all, *The President's Daughter*, about how she and Harding had sex in a White House coat closet and had a daughter together. Harding's family refused to support the daughter after his death. Peter Swann knows all this. So does Avery, though she pretends not to.

Peter's big idea is to hug and kiss to keep warm. Smooth, Avery thinks. But it works, she has to admit. She wants campus to clear out, for everyone else to disappear. It's not like they're making out, just long hugs with close-mouthed lip-pecks. Anything more than that would be totally embarrassing PDA. But as long as they do to each other only what they're doing to everyone else, they can call it *practice.*

Avery assumes they'll go back to her room, but when their shift ends, they go to D-hall for dinner and end up sitting with other people, and that breaks the spell, though Avery catches Peter looking at her, and this feels good to Avery — to share a secret.

Her mother keeps calling, and late at night, alone in her room, Avery finally answers.

"I started a Twitter account," her mother says.

Avery drops the phone and goes straight to her computer. Her mother's first tweet is a photo of herself wearing the blue tie. Well, not *that* blue tie — how would she ever have gotten it back — but she bought the same one and has kept it all these years.

Avery picks up the phone, but her mother is gone. She calls her mother back, but no answer. She leaves a message: "Take. It. Down. Now."

She keeps checking the Twitter feed until

she falls asleep.

As soon as she wakes, just before midnight, she checks again. The photo is gone.

In its place is another tweet: *Happy V Day to the love of my life.*

Don't start tweeting about *him,* Avery thinks. Please don't start doing crazy shit.

And then a new tweet appears: *Was talking about my daughter by the way. Hugs and kisses baby.*

She changed her name, a symbol of starting over, separating past from present, and yet secretly she wants to tell someone her story. She lies awake in her dorm room, periodically checking her mother's Twitter feed. Nothing new — not yet. My mother probably wants to out me, she thinks. Payback for changing my name. She imagines telling David the whole story, but she knows that he wouldn't understand. Then again, maybe that would make him the perfect audience: she would get to tell her story, and then it would be forgotten. She wonders, maybe because she spent part of the day with him, about Peter Swann, if she might tell him the truth someday, but as soon as she imagines beginning her story — she's not sure where she'd begin, maybe with the photo of the man and the baby, still in her pocket, maybe with the blue tie, maybe with the files on her computer, the part of the story before she was born — she thinks: No way, I don't trust anyone.

MARCH 1, 2010

Betsy doesn't watch scary movies, never has, not like her brother with his Stephen King obsession, which drove their mother nuts, but she's seen enough, usually through the spaces between her fingers, to know that when you hear noises in the night, and your fiancé is asleep beside you, you don't get out of bed, certainly not alone, to investigate.

But that's what she does, just like those soon-dead fools in slasher films.

In the hallway, she hears it again.

Not a whisper, not a door creaking, not footsteps.

More like flapping, something flying.

Slowly, not fully awake, in that sleepy state she likes best, she walks toward Nick's room, what used to be his, empty now except for two yoga mats and a cushion Cal sits on when he meditates. For years the bed remained, the dresser, the rug, a small bookcase, a shelf of trophies. Jackets hung on hooks on the wall. Even after her mother was gone, her father kept Nick's room as it had been. For a long time he didn't touch her mother's things either, not a sweater in her dresser, not a pair of shoes in the closet, not a book on her nightstand. Sentimental gestures change nothing, Betsy thinks, but what else can we do?

She hesitates at the door, hand on the knob, listening.

She hears it again — what she assumes is a bat. She opens the door and turns on the dim sconce lamp on the wall. She sees that the windows are open. This surprises her: it's been a cold week, and Cal never forgets to close down the house at night, the way her father used to when she was a girl. She steps farther into the room. She isn't sure if it would be better to leave the door open so she can leave easily or close it behind her so that the bat, if that's what she heard, can't go somewhere else in the house. She decides to close the door.

Then she sees something fly across the room and land on her yoga mat. She can't see what it is, but it flew more like a bird than a bat. She moves closer, careful not to frighten it, and then she sits on the mat, a few feet away from what she can now see, almost impossible to believe, is a cardinal. She doesn't know much about cardinals but guesses that it's highly unusual for one to be standing so close to a human on a cold night in a Philadelphia brownstone. She thinks of Nick because his high school football team was the Cardinals — he was always wearing something with a cardinal on it, a hat or jersey or sweatshirt — and as she sits on the mat, she feels both heavy and light, she closes her eyes, and a peace comes over her, the way it does whenever she feels Nick and imagines he's watching her.

She hears her name. She opens her eyes, sees Cal in the doorway. She doesn't remember having fallen asleep, but hours must have passed. It's still dark, but morning. Cal is coming in to meditate. He's happy. Betsy can tell that he thinks she's been meditating, that she felt well enough, motivated enough, to get up early, before even he was up.

When someone you love is happy about something not true — Betsy has not been meditating, she has not felt motivated or well — is it better to let him be happy and not know the truth or to tell him the truth

81

and make him unhappy? Something tells her that it would ruin Cal's morning were she to say, "I fell asleep in here hours ago," true or not. By saying that, she would worry him more than he's already worried about her. No one, especially not Cal, has used the word *breakdown* to describe what Betsy has been going through, what prompted her to take a leave of absence from the foundation and move back to Philadelphia. But that word comes to her now — oddly, after such a peaceful feeling and a sleep so deep she's not sure time has actually passed. The cardinal is gone.

Cal bends down to kiss her on the lips, just long enough to express love and attraction without soliciting sex. She stands and hugs him. She likes the way his eyes don't quite open all the way in the morning. She likes that his hair, a buzz cut since he was fifteen, looks the same in the morning as any time of the day. Whenever she closes her eyes and touches his hair, as she does now, he seems very much the same man she met almost six years ago. She likes that he sleeps shirtless — the least *Cal* thing he does. That must sound like a backhanded compliment, she thinks, maybe even an insult, to say that she likes most the thing he does that's most unlike him to do. But it's more that she likes when he surprises her.

"Did you open the windows?"

"No," she says.

"I closed them last night."

"Are you sure?"

"Pretty sure."

When Cal is sure about something, as he often seems to be, he says so. From Cal, *pretty sure* means *not so sure,* and it disappoints her that he probably left the window open; she wants to believe that something magical happened.

He puts one hand on her face and the other on her belly. She knows it's crazy, but she thinks he knows, or that by touching her belly he will come to know, so she moves his hand. They stand in Nick's old room looking at each other. She almost tells him then — he has this way of staring at her that makes it difficult to hide — but she kisses him again and doesn't stop until the urge to tell has passed.

Maybe it's the Nick-feeling — the sense that he's close and watching — that prompts Betsy to pull a box of photos out from the attic later that morning. Probably not the greatest idea, she thinks. She noticed the box when she helped her father move into the facility in Buchanan. She hates that word, *facility,* it sounds so clinical, and it reminds her that her father no longer has the *facilities* he once had, and neither does she — to run her mother's foundation, to visit her father, to know how to *be* around him. She hasn't had *that* facility — knowing how to be around her father — in years; but at least she'd been able to fake it, sometimes.

She's thought about the box from time to time but hasn't touched it until now. Cal is at work, so she brings the box down to the bedroom — she still can't help but think of it as her parents' room — and places it on the bed. It's a vintage leather hatbox with a white rope handle, and inside, in no order — no labeled envelopes or rubber-banded stacks — are a hundred or so photos, some faceup, some facedown. Even before reaching in, she can see herself as a girl, Nick as a baby, her father — unbelievable, she thinks — with a handle-bar mustache. Seeing Nick as a baby, and her father's mustache — which actually looks not so bad on him — makes her smile, and she decides that this exercise in sentimentality — if that's what it is — might make her feel better, or at least might not make her feel worse. She wonders, as she reaches into the box and touches the photos, if that's what she had wanted: to feel worse. To bring whatever she's been feeling, her paralyzing ambivalence (marriage, pregnancy, father), her low-level sadness living in this house again, to an emotional head, like putting a hot compress on a whitehead — she's been breaking out lately for the first time since high school — in order to bring all the pus — what her mother used to call *poison* — to the surface, so that you can then squeeze it and, after pain that brings tears to your eyes, be done with it. Maybe that's what she had in mind, but now she feels that this is going to be okay. Nick in his football uniform. Her father with a mustache. No problem.

She moves her hand around in the photos as if this were a lottery or raffle drawing. Inside the box, she is a baby and a high school student; her parents are newlyweds; her brother is alive. In a linear timeline, as in life, there is cause and effect, this leads to that leads to that, and so on, there are ramifications for one's choices, what would the world be without that; but inside the hatbox, where time is not a line, the past is never quite dead, you can go back, forward, back again. You can't change anything —

except the order. You can end wherever you want.

She closes her eyes and takes out one of her favorite photos, her mother at sixteen, a few years before she met David. It isn't only that her mother is pretty with her bob cut and bangs, her short-sleeved black-and-white plaid dress, her black clutch purse; it's more that she looks so happy — happier than Betsy ever saw her. Maybe as you get older, Betsy thinks, you become less happy. It must have been sunny that day: her mother is squinting at whoever is taking the picture. Maybe some high school boyfriend, Betsy thinks. You smile that way only at someone you're in love with.

She's smiling that way on her wedding day too — the next photo Betsy happens to take out of the box. So is her father, who is wearing a black jacket with tails, gray slacks, a gray five-button vest, and a dark gray silk tie (this was before he wore only blue ties). Her mother's dress is elegant, with a short, modest veil, the kind of wedding dress Betsy chose for herself.

The longer Betsy stares at the photo, her okay feeling, the nostalgia-induced fantasy that the moment captured in the photo is permanent, gives way to the reality of the timeline: it is 2010, not 1966, and in between, forty-four years have happened. This is a hatbox, this photo is made of paper, this is her bedroom now. She looks at the photo and thinks: They had no idea. If she could dive into that box and swim around in time, if she could be there on her parents' wedding day, she might say to them: "Be careful, take care of each other, hold on tightly, remember this moment, don't lose your way, don't lose each other." But even were she to give them this advice, even were she to tell them exactly what was to come, would they have changed their minds? Would they have not gone through with it? Would they have parted ways? Would they have said, "We don't" rather than "We do"? Or would they have disbelieved it? Would they have said, "Not us — never in a million years"? Or would they have believed it *was* possible but looked at each other and said, "We'll figure a way out — we'll cheat fate"?

Too much. No more.

She puts the photo back into the box and covers the box with its lid.

But then she thinks, One more, I can't end with this feeling, and so she opens the box, reaches in, and pulls out — God, why *this* one?

She has seen this image so often online

that she's surprised to see the actual photo. Her mother is thin, too thin, but still pretty. Her parents are in profile. Her father's hands are on her mother's face, hers on his. Her father's wedding ring is clearly visible. Her mother is looking up at him, but his eyes are closed. Her expression seems loving but anguished, as if she's asking *why*. They look as if they're trying to hold on to each other, to hold each other up.

But just as the photo of her parents' wedding day triggered sadness rather than happiness, this photo, taken during one of the most difficult times of their lives, triggers in Betsy feelings she didn't expect: she feels sorry for them. They do love each other, she can see it, and they are trying to hold on.

No more.

She puts the photo into the box, brings the box back to the attic, and returns to where she is on the timeline of her life: March 1, 2010. She has no idea what to do with the rest of this day, this life.

Avery bikes across campus and then through cold, gray Buchanan, Pennsylvania, a college town of old row homes and churches and too many bars. Just outside town, on either side of the road she bikes every

Monday and Wednesday, are farms awaiting spring, land so flat she might as well be in Iowa. She forgot to wear gloves, and by the time she arrives, her hands are dry and nearly numb from wind. Her nose is running. It looks as if she's been crying.

As soon as David sees her, he whispers, "We have work to do today."

"What kind?"

"The female vote," he says. "Shaking hands, kissing babies."

Then he seems confused, more confused than Avery. "Where are all the babies?" he says.

"Don't worry," she says. "Babies can't vote."

"But people who like photos of babies — they vote."

"What are you running for?"

He laughs as if Avery has made a joke.

"Do you know how to tie a tie?" he asks, as if he hasn't asked her this every time she has come to see him, and as if every time she hasn't said no, sorry, she doesn't.

A blue tie is on his lap, but he's shaking too much to grasp it. His hand is like the mechanical claw in that impossible carnival game where you lower a crane and try to steady it enough and open the claw just at the right moment to snag a stuffed bear made in China.

He keeps trying but can't grab the tie, so Avery picks it up. But she has no idea what to do next.

She pushes David's wheelchair in front of the mirror on the inside of the door and stands behind him. She lifts his collar and tries her best, but David laughs.

"Hold on, hold on," he whispers. "Pull the wide part down."

Behind him, her arms resting on David's shoulders, Avery pulls the wide part down. She watches her reflection. If she weren't holding the tie, she thinks, if instead she crossed her arms on his chest and laid her head on one of his shoulders, or touched the front of her head to the back of his, they'd be in an embrace. Avery waits for further instruction, thinking about the word *embrace,* which is more than a hug, as far as she's concerned. Two people about to part for a long time, or two people reunited after a long time apart, don't hug; they embrace. She imagines two people enclosing one another, bracing against each other. Two people in desperate love or crushed by the same grief.

"Who is Dave?" he says.

"I don't know," she says.

"Am I Dave?"

"You're David."

"Then who's Dave?"

She reminds him about the tie — that she needs help.

"Cross the wide end over the narrow end," he says. "Now, loop it under and around. Good, good. Now around again at the top. No, at the top. Start to make the knot. Like that — good. Now up through the loop."

She does what David tells her to do. She pulls the narrow end down while pushing the knot up, then slips the narrow end through the small white loop stitched to the back of the wide end.

Avery doesn't need a father or brother to know how a belt works. She's worn belts. She's unbuckled the belts of a few boys and watched others unbuckle their own. She slides David's belt through the loops on one side, then reaches around his back to feel for the loops she can't see, then passes the belt from one hand to the other, her face pressed against the tie she just tied.

This is almost a hug, she thinks.

"Now if only we had some babies," David says.

"How about you just shake some hands."

"All my hands do is shake."

"Maybe you could go around and introduce yourself."

"Hello, my name is David — David what?"

"Christie."

"Hey, that's a good name."

In the community room, women in wheelchairs play basketball. They take turns trying to shoot a pink plastic ball through a kiddie hoop a few feet away.

"The female vote," Avery says.

They watch the game. There seem to be no rules and at the end there's no winner. The ladies who can applaud, applaud. A staff member, a heavy man not much older than Avery, takes away the hoop and ball.

Avery pushes David's chair to the center of the room. "I'm here today to listen to you," he says, but no one looks up.

"They can't hear," Avery says.

"Are they deaf?"

"Possibly," she says, "but what I mean is, you whisper."

"Are you sure?"

"You just did it again."

David looks confused, as if he doesn't believe her.

"I can speak for you, if you want."

"How will you know what to say?"

"You be Cyrano, I'll be Christian."

"My wife used to read that to my daughter," he says.

"Tell me what to say."

"Hello, my name is David Christie, and I would like to earn your vote."

"Hello," Avery says, and waits for the ladies to look. "This is David Christie, and he would like to earn your vote."

■ ■ ■ ■

PART THREE:
MISTAKES WERE
MADE

1991–1992

■ ■ ■ ■

AUGUST 1991

Iowa. It was all about Iowa.

David's campaign headquarters was in Old City, Philadelphia. Liberty Bell, Independence Hall, Ben Franklin, Founding Fathers, Declaration of Independence — perfect associations for someone running for president, his campaign manager told him. But he pretty much lived in Iowa. He spent time in New Hampshire too, and Maine, and South Dakota, and Maryland. And DC, of course. There was still the Senate — committees, votes, that glacial pace he hated. Posturing, ass-kissing, backstabbing, bullshit. And there was home — Center City, Delancey Place, Danielle and Betsy. But he was rarely there, not nearly as often as he'd promised he'd be.

No — it was about Iowa. Small, bouncy planes, shitty motels, six or seven events a day, churches and schools and corn boils and ice cream socials, sixteen-hour days, only to do it again the next day, and the next. It was all about Iowa.

Everyone else had left — Tsongas and Clinton and Kerrey and Brown. No chance to win after Governor Kirkwood announced, but David stayed. People said he was nuts, what a waste of time and money, but he didn't care — he was staying. He had a plan: he was going to show that he didn't give up, and that would become the story. He'd wait for Kirkwood to make a mistake, he'd sneak up on him, and by then it would be too late for the others, they'd be long gone, their Iowa campaigns reduced to lawn signs. Not David — for him it was Iowa or bust. And the good thing was he didn't even have to win. Close would be as good as a win. But if he won — shit. That was why it was all about Iowa. There would be no New Hampshire or Maine or South Dakota or anywhere without Iowa. *Iowa* had become a mantra, a word David spoke and wrote and thought so often it had become a sound, a feeling: *Iowa.* The feeling was he was going to win. He was still a speck in the polls — Kirkwood was Iowa born and raised, his father a coal miner, lost his mother young, grew up in a house without running water, high school in West Des

Moines, Iowa State University, navy jet pilot — but never mind all that, David was determined to win. He wasn't sure how, but he could feel it. He had recurring dreams of standing alone in bright, almost blinding sunlight in vast fields of brown cornstalks. Just him — no one else. The last one standing.

But he woke one August morning in the Hotel Fort Des Moines, his home away from home, gripped with doubt — not about winning, but about why he wanted to win, why he was there so far from his family. He looked in the bathroom mirror and didn't recognize himself. Was there more gray in his hair? Had his eyebrows become bushier? Was that a stray hair growing from his ear? He looked older, shorter, softer, he thought. He dropped for fifty-two push-ups to match his age. He did this every day, but this morning, panicked, he did them too quickly and had to break them into two sets. Even so, not too shabby. He stood, took off his T-shirt, and looked in the mirror again. He hardened his stomach, flexed his biceps. That was better. He looked forty-two, not fifty-two. There wasn't more gray in his hair, after all. His eyebrows looked fine.

Usually his body man and traveling chief of staff, Tim Swisher, ran with him, but today David wanted to be alone. That was the only thing he ever chewed Tim out about — when he needed to be alone. Someone was always following him, always hovering — lobbyists and party bosses and policy chiefs and media gurus and all the hired killers — and sometimes he thought, Enough already, give me some space, let me breathe. Poor Tim, he was the one David would bark at even when it was someone else crowding him. It was Tim's job to clear space. It was his job to shield David. It was his job to know what David needed before he asked for it. It was his job to know David Christie better than David Christie knew himself. It was his job to know everything except what David didn't want him to know. And if he happened to know something David didn't want him to know, it was his job to pretend not to know it. He knew more than anyone, but no one could know more than David, who made sure that not quite everything came to him through Tim. That was fine with Tim; he trusted David. So if Tim heard David leave his hotel room earlier than usual that morning — Tim was almost certainly awake; he slept only a few hours a night yet was always sharp — he must have known not to open his door, he must have known that David wanted to be alone.

It was too early to be hot, but David could feel it — it was going to be a scorcher of a day, ninety-something, maybe triple digits, record-breaking hot. And humid. Which David hated even more than heat. Humidity made him sweat like an Iowa pig — not that pigs actually sweat — and made him irritable, which he couldn't afford to be, ever, because he had to smile and shake hands and pretend that every person he met was the most important person on the planet.

Not even a mile into his run alongside the Des Moines River — a half-dozen diehards fishing off the bridge — and already he was tired and uncomfortable and angry with the day — with everything. He didn't want to be running this morning, yet here he was. He didn't want to be in Des Moines, yet here he was. He couldn't remember why he was running for president except that someone told him he should, and that he could win, and then *People* magazine named him one of the "50 most beautiful people in the world," and before he set one foot in the state, the polls said that 30 percent of Iowans recognized his face, if not his name, and that was good enough, and here he was — the goddamn state fair today.

No, it was too late to turn back now. Once David was in, whatever it was, he didn't like to lose. He was running. So he kept running.

Normally he ran three or four loops, more if he felt good, but today he didn't want the river and the men waiting for a nibble, half-asleep with their legs dangling over the water. His legs were burning and his lungs were burning and his eyes were burning from sweat and his shirt was sticking to his chest, and he said screw this. After one loop, soaked, he took off his shirt and ran downtown.

A few blocks from the state capitol he saw some kid, probably a college student, taking down a Christie sign from a telephone pole and replacing it with a Kirkwood sign. David stopped running. As the kid was taping the sign, he must have sensed David behind him. He turned around.

"Can I help you?"

"Yes," David said, "you can stop touching what belongs to me."

It didn't register at first — the kid looked about to mouth off — but then he seemed to recognize David.

"Put it back up," David said.

"Sorry I took down your sign," the kid said when he was finished.

"You're sorry you got caught."

"Just doing my job."

"Okay, but you're working for the wrong guy." David's face — his face on the poster — had a smudge of dirt on it, so he licked his finger and wiped it clean. "Listen," David said, "when it's down to me and Bush, I'd appreciate your vote. And if you come to your senses before then, give me a call."

David smiled and offered his hand, and the kid shook it, and David kept eye contact — he was good at that — and if Iowa had been a primary rather than a caucus, if this kid's vote could have been private, David believed he could have won him over. He ran away into the humid August morning. He was angry with Iowa and the world and the last thing he wanted to do was eat fried food on a stick while listening to Garth Brooks.

A few hours later, that was exactly what he was doing. Deep-fried cheese on a stick, deep-fried hot dog on a stick, deep-fried pickle on a stick, deep-fried corndog on a stick. People kept handing David sticks, and he kept eating, and at some point he stopped asking what it was. Nothing hot on a stick could make him hotter than he already was, which was the hottest he'd ever been.

How are you? Nice to see you. I'm David Christie, we could use your support. David Christie, nice to meet you, we could use your help. Hi, I'm David Christie. Hi, good to see you, we'd really like you to give us a chance. I keep saying *we* and *us* because it's not about me, it's about all of us who want to see things change. Hello, David Christie, nice to meet you. We'd love your support. Hi, I'm David. David, hello, nice to see you. David Christie, David Christie, David Christie, hello. I'd like to have the chance to earn your vote.

He hated this. He preferred one-on-one, but Tim reminded him that the fair was all about see-me-touch-me. "They just want to shake your hand," Tim said. "Actually, they just want to be able to *say* that they shook your hand, that you said hi, that they were close to you."

David Christie, nice to meet you. Thank you very much, appreciate that. I won't disappoint you. That's what I'm going to do when I'm president. David Christie, I'd like to earn your support. I'll tell you the truth even if it's something you may not want to hear. Hi, David Christie, I'm running for president of the United States. Nice to see you, thanks for coming out. I'm tired of two Americas, one for the haves, one for the

104

have-nots, one for the insiders, one for the outsiders. We need one America. Hi there, nice to see you. Beautiful child. David Christie, appreciate your support.

People kept coming at him, and he kept smiling and shaking hands, and he was starting to find a rhythm, he was starting to remember that he believed what he was saying. But the damn heat — he could hardly breathe. Men in bib overalls pushed massive gourds in wheelbarrows. Pigs grunted in their pens. David couldn't avoid the smell of chickens and cows and manure. He was swept up a hill away from the fairgrounds but could still hear Garth Brooks. Someone handed David funnel cake and he got powdered sugar on his pants. He paused for a milk chug-a-lug and a grape-stomping contest and arm-wrestled a high school kid. Children wearing helmets and masks rode rodeo on sheep. A boy, maybe ten, shorts at his ankles, peed behind a bale of hay. And David thought, as he shook sweaty hands: Why are they alive when he's not? Why are these people breathing and eating here in East Jesus when my son is gone?

"Tim, get me some water, would you?"

"You doing all right?"

"I just need some water, okay?"

Tim came back with a bottle of water, and

David drank it. Then they continued up the hill, a small crowd following, to where gourds were being weighed.

Halfway up the hill, David heard, "Help!" — a woman's voice. When he turned around, he saw a woman standing above a boy — the same boy he'd seen peeing behind a bale of hay. The boy was shaking in the dirt as if possessed. A half-dozen people stood watching; they seemed afraid to touch him. David knelt in the dirt beside him and cradled his head. The boy's jaw locked and spit flew out of his mouth and his eyes rolled back, and this was the first real thing David had experienced in weeks.

A minute passed, a minute that seemed much longer, and the boy's legs stopped jerking. His face relaxed. His mouth fell open.

"I don't know what's happening," his mother said. "This has never happened before."

The boy seemed almost too calm, his mouth too slack. His eyes were open but empty. David put his ear to the boy's mouth. He asked everyone to be quiet, and waited to feel the boy breathing. Nothing. He felt the neck for a pulse — nothing. He checked again, made sure, and then started CPR. The boy's mother said, "God, please," just once, and then she was quiet, everyone was, as David breathed into the boy's mouth and pressed his chest and breathed into his mouth again, and it was as if there were no one else in the world except him and this boy.

The boy breathed so suddenly — a gasp while David's mouth was touching his — that it scared David. He sat there, dirt on his pants, his shirt soaked with sweat, and cradled the boy's head until paramedics arrived. Then he hugged the boy's mother as she cried on his shoulder.

NOVEMBER 1991

Two months ago he couldn't remember why he was running — he was hot and sweaty and old and some Kirkwood punk was ripping down his face from a pole — but then he breathed life back into a boy at the state fair and the boy breathed life into David's campaign. Two photos — David cradling the boy's head, about to start CPR, and David embracing the mother — appeared on the front page of the *Des Moines Register* and the *Washington Post* and the *New York Times* and most newspapers in the country. The bump was way more than a bump: it kept going and going, and now David was down by only single digits in Iowa and had pulled even in New Hampshire and in national polls. Kirkwood could hear him coming now, David thought. Tsongas and Clinton could hear him. Bush too.

Some days he still wasn't sure why he was

running, but it was better not to think about it too much. He cared about the issues he'd built his campaign around — closing the increasing gap between wealthy and poor Americans; raising the level of honesty and transparency in government; recommitting to the importance of serving one's country — but everyone knew, and now he knew, that running for president was a sadomasochistic affair. But after what happened with the boy, David decided: Fuck it, who cares, I'm not going to stop long enough to think about it, I'm going to wake up each day, most in Iowa, get in the car, and let Tim tell me where we're going — diner, pizza place, flapjack festival — and what the other candidates are doing, what the press is saying, what happened in the world overnight, then get out of the car and smile and shake hands and answer questions and ask people how they're doing and really pay attention and have fun.

He went for a long run on a clear, cold morning two days before Thanksgiving. Only one man was out fishing in the Des Moines — a short, stocky, bearded man with a Cubs cap pulled down over his eyes and a hole in the back of his coat. The man could have been sleeping, but David paused his run to ask him if anything was biting

(David had never been fishing in his life).

Without looking at David, the man said, "Not yet."

David held out his hand and said, "My name is David Christie, and I'm running for president of the United States."

The man shook his hand. "I know who you are."

"I'd appreciate it if you'd give me a chance."

"I like Kirkwood."

"I like him too," David said. "Seems like a nice guy. But that doesn't mean he should be president."

"Why should you?"

"Because I'm not afraid."

"Everyone's afraid of something."

"What I mean is, I'm not afraid of any*one* — lobbyists and special interest groups and people who think they can throw their money around to get what they want."

The man spat into the water and wiggled his line. "Funny, you're the first I ever heard say that."

"I *mean* it."

"And you're the first I ever heard say *that.*"

"That's why I'm running. I want things to change."

The man lifted the brim of his hat and

gave David a look.

"I know, I know," David said, "I'm the first you ever heard say that."

The man smiled and went back to his fishing. "What you did with that boy — even if you don't win, you'll always have that."

"I was happy for his mother."

"I lost a child years ago — my daughter."

"I'm very sorry," David said. "I know what that feels like."

"Cherry pit," he said. "I tried everything, I tried so hard I broke her ribs, but couldn't get it up."

"I lost my son in an accident."

"We use that word, *lost,* but we're never going to find them."

"No," David said, "we're not."

He thanked the man for his time, wished him luck fishing, then ran around the river. Flurries began to fall — the first snow of the season.

On a cold Friday night, the day after Thanksgiving, Danielle was in New York City, hours after having met with her oncologist. She looked at the young woman walking beside her and recognized the blue dress she was wearing — it used to be Danielle's — but not, at first, the young woman: Betsy looked like a younger Danielle, and the dress only heightened this perception.

"Take your pill."

"Later, okay?"

"Why are you so stubborn?"

"I'm not stubborn," Danielle said. "I have cancer, and therefore I can have whatever I want, and what I want is to see this play without being loopy."

Betsy was right — she *could* be stubborn. When Danielle's stomach cancer was diagnosed in September, David said he would end his campaign, and Betsy seemed to want this too, her parents in the same place, but Danielle said absolutely not. She meant it but was also aware that it was the selfless response and would be seen as such. Normally she didn't care much how others saw her, but she was scared, and maybe being seen as brave would actually make her so. Betsy, a senior in high school, wanted to defer college for a year, and Danielle said the same to her — absolutely not — but Betsy fought her on it, fought harder than Danielle expected her to, it wasn't just a gesture, and she grudgingly admired — and was moved by — her daughter's unwillingness to budge. Danielle had said, "Let's see where we are in the spring. A lot can happen between now and then."

David had bought three tickets for *Six*

Degrees of Separation, a play Danielle had seen alone over a year ago when it was Off-Broadway. It was a tragicomedy, and Danielle had been considering a new course on this subject, and she'd wanted to see it again. David had wanted to see it too, but: Iowa. The play was nearing the end of its Broadway run. She'd loved it the first time she saw it, in a smaller theater — so small that the cast, when not onstage, sat in the front row. She hoped the director would keep that touch, which must have been born out of spatial restrictions but fit organically with a play that broke the fourth wall. Maybe she could offer an entire course on plays that broke the fourth wall. She stopped walking a few blocks from Lincoln Center, took out the hand-size spiral notebook she always brought with her to the theater, and made a note: *new courses: tragicomedy, fourth wall.*

"You're not going to take notes during the play, are you?" Betsy said.

"Of course not."

Danielle flipped to the first pages, where she'd written the following as soon as *Six Degrees* ended and the lights came on the first time she saw it:

Stockard Channing Stockard Channing Stockard Channing

Tell them!

Eureka in the bathtub.

Whatever's going on anywhere, I do not want to know. I don't want to know. I don't want to know.

How do we keep the experience?

It's pained on two sides.

She read this last line three times, once aloud — not realizing that she was spoiling the final line of the play for Betsy — before she noticed her mistake. She corrected it: *It's painted on two sides.*

She put the notebook back into her purse, and they continued to walk toward the theater.

"I can tell you're in pain, your lips are tight."

"I'm okay," Danielle said.

"Seriously, just take a pill."

"You look pretty."

"Don't change the subject," Betsy said.

"Stunning, actually."

"Because I've lost weight."

"Not as much as I have."

"I'm determined to fatten you up."

Danielle winced, stopped walking, and grabbed her side.

"That's it — you're taking one."

"I don't need one."

"Obviously you do."

"Then I don't *want* one."

"Take half."

Danielle forced a smile. "How much longer until you leave for college?"

"I told you, I'm deferring."

"I told you, you're not."

"Dad says it's my decision."

"Mom says it's not."

Danielle started to walk again, slowly, but Betsy stayed where she was. Danielle stopped and looked back, waited for Betsy to catch up.

"I'll make you a deal," Danielle said. "I take the pill, you agree not to defer."

"I don't even understand you. It's almost like you *want* to be in pain."

Danielle winced again, she doubled over this time, but before Betsy could say anything she waved her off and said, "I'm fine, I'm fine."

What she wanted to say: "Yes, I want this pain. I don't want to die, but I accept this pain, because I had four glasses of wine, and I was behind the wheel, and I have been waiting for this — call it karma, call it penance."

But she could never say that. That wouldn't work in a play, she thought — a character saying that to another character. Maybe it could work if spoken directly to the audience — right through the fourth wall.

Betsy hugged her mother, and as she did, she reached into her mother's purse. She took out the pill bottle, opened it, shook one pill into her hand, and gave it to her mother.

Danielle put the pill into her mouth.

Betsy returned the bottle to her mother's purse, and they walked the final block to the theater.

Once inside, Danielle went into the restroom, found an open stall, closed the door behind her, spit the pill into the toilet, and flushed.

They found their seats — fifth row center. Ten minutes more. It was strange to have Betsy — to have anyone — sitting beside her. She preferred to see plays alone; it was one of her greatest pleasures. She didn't like sharing this experience, not even with people she loved, even though that was one of the main points of theater. Once the lights went down, she liked to imagine that she was alone. Everything around her would fade away; so would she. It's the strangest, most wonderful thing in the world, she thought — human beings on a stage, acting out a drama made of words written by another human being, so that other human beings can witness — *pay* to witness — a dramatic journey that causes them to feel things they might not otherwise, or to feel more deeply what they already feel.

This, she would miss. David, of course, and Betsy. But more than anything but them, she would miss *this*. If there is an afterlife, she thought, let there be theater. Let there be Nick, please. And theater. All the world's a stage, as Shakespeare put it, so maybe being dead meant that you spent eternity as a ghost, watching an infinite number of human dramas play out.

She felt Betsy's hand on hers on the armrest between them, and this surprised her — that she was alive, that her daughter was with her. She looked at their hands touching and decided that hands were miracles. She held Betsy's tightly. They had become closer in the two months Danielle had been sick, but they had been growing closer even before that, especially with David away in DC during the week — and increasingly on weekends — for the past seven years, from the time Betsy was ten, and now gone even more, and farther away, with the presidential campaign.

The lights in the theater flickered. That thrill never got old for Danielle.

"Don't tell your father," she said.

"Don't tell him what?"

"What my oncologist said."

"Mom, I don't like secrets."

"I'll tell him after Iowa, promise."

"The doctor didn't say it's worse, just not better."

"Not better *is* worse."

"I know you didn't swallow your pill, by the way."

Danielle laughed. "You're very annoying."

"It's only codeine."

"Those pills make me drowsy, and I want to enjoy this play — this matters to me."

"Well, you matter to me," Betsy said.

"You're very sweet," Danielle said.

"Okay, but I still want you to take a pill."

"Sweetheart, please."

"I'll leave."

"What happened to the old Betsy?"

"The fat one."

"You were never fat."

"The chunky one."

"Sweetheart."

"The one who used to be afraid of you."

"You were never afraid of me," Danielle said. She stared at Betsy, and saw that she was serious. "Well, that makes me feel awful." She took out the pill bottle, shook out a pill, put it into her mouth, waited for it to soften on her tongue, and then swallowed it.

They sat there quietly for a minute.

"Betsy," Danielle said, "I'm sorry you were afraid of me."

"I'm not anymore."

"I'm sorry you ever were," Danielle said. "You shouldn't be afraid of your mother."

"It's okay now," Betsy said.

The lights flickered again, and then the theater went dark.

"I'm still not lying to Dad," Betsy whispered.

"We'll talk about that later," Danielle said.

High above the stage an imitation Kandinsky revolved; it was painted on both sides. One side was wild and brightly colored; the other side was colder, more geometric. The painting kept revolving, and then it stopped: the geometric painting faced the audience.

Then a middle-aged couple ran onto the stage wearing silk robes, and the woman, played by Stockard Channing, said to her husband, "Tell them!"

DECEMBER 1991

Two hundred people waited for David in the gymnasium, and he was already twenty minutes late. Tim was obsessed with staying on schedule, but the truth was David wasn't in the mood to stump. He went to bed with the stump speech in his head, he woke hearing it, and in between he dreamed about it. It had become so rote that the only way for him to *feel* the stump, and he needed to, was to go off script. Winging it came with risks and rewards, but fuck it. He made a sudden detour off the path to the high school's entrance and headed for the football field, where the team was practicing.

Tim followed. "Senator," he said, but David didn't respond. "Senator, come on."

"Just a few minutes."

"We're late."

"Just a few."

"It's starting to snow."

"So what?"

"David, come on," he said, but David removed his jacket and handed it to Tim.

He walked across the football field and joined the huddle. The players stared at him. "Hey, hey, hey," the coach said.

"Mind if I take a few snaps?"

"This is a closed practice."

"My name's David Christie."

He recognized David then and shook his hand. "Mike Leader," he said.

"Great name for a football coach."

"Or a president."

"You're not thinking about running, are you?"

"No, thank you."

"My son used to play football back in Pennsylvania."

"You sure you want to play in those shoes?"

"They're the only shoes I have."

The coach told the receivers to line up, but no one moved. "Come on!" he said, and blew the whistle hanging from a rope around his neck.

The first kid ran a skinny post, the kind of route over the middle that gets you a concussion, and David hit him easy. The second kid ran a post pattern twenty yards downfield, and David's pass was a step behind him, but the kid reached back for the ball and made David look good. The third kid ran a flare, and David pumped, and the kid turned it into a wheel up the sideline, and David hit him in stride. The fourth kid, tall and skinny, all legs, a body better suited for basketball, turned on the burners, a go pattern, nothing but speed, and David threw as far as he could — forty yards, not bad. The kid had to slow down to catch the ball, but not too much, and then he high-stepped into the end zone and spiked the ball, and the other boys clapped, and the coach said, "You busy on Saturday?"

David's shoulder was sore, he'd have to ice it, but the receivers kept running their routes and he kept throwing. A few dying quails — there was a joke somewhere in there about the vice president, he thought — but mostly strikes. It was snowing harder and David's socks were soaked and his shirt had come undone, its tail flapping behind him, but he didn't care. Then he noticed that Tim — ever-resourceful Tim — had brought out the press. They shot video of David.

When his shoulder was near dead, he packed a snowball and threw it at Tim — right in the back. Then he went after the press. They hid behind their cameras and packed their own snowballs and threw them at David, and it was six against one, but David held his own, and this too was caught on video.

Before David gave his stump speech inside the high school, Tim told him, "That was *great*. You looked athletic, spontaneous, a guy unafraid to ruin his loafers." But David thought, I was just throwing a football like I used to with Nick on cold, snowy Pennsylvania Saturdays before games.

That night, back at the Hotel Fort Des Moines, when he was in his room, finally alone, the phone rang.

"I was wondering when you were going to call," David said, before he knew who it was.

It was Betsy calling to wish him a happy birthday. He'd forgotten, but pretended otherwise.

"How was your day?" she said.

"Good day," David said. "Played some football. Had a snowball fight."

"Don't have too much fun without us."

"I miss you guys."

"How much longer do we have to do this?"

"Not a day longer than we have to."

"Mom's sleeping, but she said happy birthday."

"Tell her I love her, okay?"

"Who's there with you?"

"That's just the TV."

"Go to sleep."

"You're the boss."

"Good night," she said. "I love you."

"I love you too," David said.

Her mother was too sick from chemotherapy to travel to New Hampshire for the debate. She told Betsy that *she* should go, but Betsy didn't want to leave her mother alone. Her father said he would miss them, and it would help just to know they were watching at home.

They sat on the couch together, her mother under a wool blanket Betsy had covered her with, and watched the debate on TV. Her father against Bill Clinton, Paul Tsongas, Jerry Brown, and Lee Kirkwood. Betsy was nervous, but her mother didn't seem to be; maybe the cancer treatments didn't allow her to be anything but tired.

Her father mentioned them in his opening statement — that they were unable to be there with him, but he wanted them to know that he was thinking about them. For a moment, when her father looked into the camera and said these words, Betsy thought: My father might actually become president of the United States. And he would be a good one. She was biased, she knew, and all her father had done was mention her and her mother, but she was proud of him.

Early in the debate, Tom Brokaw, the moderator, asked Governor Kirkwood if he was surprised by David Christie's rise in the polls in Iowa and if anything less than a double-digit victory in his home state would be considered a defeat.

"It's my home, but Senator Christie seems to think it's his. He's spending more time in Iowa than in Washington. Last time I checked, he still has a job there. My job is in Iowa; Senator Christie's job is running for president. He's a good politician, but make no mistake, he's a politician. He knows how to use certain events to his advantage. It's fortunate that he knows CPR, but that doesn't qualify him to be president of the United States. His entire political career has been based not on substance but on luck, to be perfectly honest. Eventually the voters of Iowa will see the truth and Senator Christie's luck will run out."

Brokaw said, "Senator Christie — your response."

"I'd prefer not to," her father said — very Bartleby of him, Betsy thought. "I concede my time to Governor Kirkwood so that he can explain how a boy having a seizure and almost dying is lucky."

"That's just like the senator to put words in my mouth," Kirkwood said. "You see, even now he's trying to use that incident — that unfortunate incident — and of course everyone is relieved that the boy is all right. I know CPR too, but I'm not using it as the center of my campaign. I'm still waiting for some substance from Senator Christie. In the short term he might get a bump from circumstances — from the media focusing on things unrelated to policy, things that cast Senator Christie in a sympathetic light — but where's the substance?"

"Senator Christie," Brokaw said.

"Thank you, Tom, but again, I concede my time back to Governor Kirkwood. I'd like to hear more about the circumstances he's referring to that make me more sympathetic. I'm not sure if he's talking about my son's death or my wife's illness or some other piece of good luck I've had."

Perhaps trying to channel Reagan, Kirkwood smiled, shook his head, and said, "There you go again — putting words in my mouth and trying to use something that — Let me say that everyone wishes Senator Christie's wife a full recovery, of course we do. But listen, I didn't bring anyone's family into this. I'm simply asking for an ounce of substance from his campaign. This is the senator's opportunity to tell us what he's running on other than his nice smile."

Brokaw turned to her father, who crossed his hands on the lectern and stared into the camera. It seemed to Betsy that her father was looking directly at her and her mother. They waited, along with everyone at the debate and everyone else watching on TV.

"Once again, I'd prefer not to respond," he said. "Governor Kirkwood is doing a fine job, without any help from me, shoving his foot very deeply into his own mouth."

The audience applauded, but her father's expression didn't change. He didn't appear angry, just strong. It was as if someone had punched him in the face, Betsy thought, and he'd hit back hard while seeming to turn the other cheek.

Ten days before Christmas and, just like that, her father was the front-runner — not just in Iowa but for the Democratic nomination.

They weren't a family big on surprises, but Betsy felt badly for her father, alone in Iowa the week before Christmas. When she and her mother showed up at his hotel room, he was so surprised that he didn't seem happy

— not happy enough, Betsy thought — to see them. He couldn't stand still; he kept walking to the window, to the bathroom, to the closet. He asked twice how the flight was; he kept saying how surprised he was.

Her mother joked that maybe he wanted them to go home, and he said it was just that he was worried about her traveling so soon after a round of chemo. "I felt much worse a few days ago, believe me," she said, "but I'm better today."

He finally hugged her, then Betsy, and then the phone rang. Four rings, a brief pause, four more rings, another pause, four more rings.

"Your people need you," her mother said.

Her father sighed before answering the phone, a sound that struck Betsy as one of frustration or exhaustion or *leave me alone already.*

Betsy could hear only her father's side of the conversation.

"That's not going to work . . . I'm afraid not . . . I know, but we can't do that . . . I understand, but . . . I have to go . . . I have to go now . . . That's correct . . . Absolutely not . . . Listen, I have to go."

As soon as he hung up the phone, he wanted to go; he rushed them out of the room before they even knew where they were going. "Hurry," he said, "before any-one else calls looking for me."

They went out to dinner, just the three of them — not counting the bodyguard who sat at the bar sipping soda. They went to a dark, gloomy Des Moines seafood restau-rant with ships' wheels and oars decorating the walls. Her mother, for the first time in weeks, had an appetite. She ate jumbo shrimp with a side of buttery asparagus, and even ordered rice pudding for dessert — though Betsy had to help her finish that. Her father was the one who didn't eat much. He ate only a few shrimp — he had ordered the same as her mother — and didn't touch his asparagus. He excused himself twice — his stomach was upset, he said — and Betsy wondered if it was the stress of the campaign.

During the walk back to the hotel, it was sleeting. Her father put his arm around her mother's waist. When she slipped, he held her up but fell himself. He sat on the sidewalk laughing, and Betsy thought: *There* you are, there's Dad.

When they got back to the room, her father had an idea. "Let's fly home together in the morning."

"I thought we'd stay here with you for a few days," her mother said.

"I'm sick of Iowa," he said.

"We just got here," Betsy said.

"I know," her father said, "but I just want to be home."

Betsy slept on a couch in the suite, and when the phone rang late in the night, her parents asleep in bed, she was the one who answered it.

"Hello?" she said. "Who's there?"

But no one was there — well, someone *was* there, but whoever it was said nothing.

Home, David and Danielle were the old David and Danielle. Or seemed to be, to Betsy. One day they all spent the entire day in their pajamas. No one said a word about Iowa. No one watched the news or read the paper or answered the phone. They made pancakes for breakfast and grilled cheese for lunch and ordered in for dinner and played board games and watched *It's a Wonderful Life,* which was on all day. Sometimes they'd begin at the end of the movie, then watch the beginning, and end somewhere in the middle. Later, they'd begin in the middle and end somewhere near the beginning. The ending was happy if they ended at the end, but sad if they ended somewhere else, like when George's father dies or when George comes home one night, snaps at his kids, then jumps off a bridge.

They were so happy to be home together that they forgot to get a tree. Betsy was the one who remembered on Christmas Eve. Her mother would have been fine picking up any old tree somewhere in South Philly, she said, but her father insisted that they cut down their own, just like every year.

They drove to the Christmas tree farm they'd been going to for years. The man who owned the farm shook her father's hand and said, "Senator, nice to see you."

"I'm still Dave to you."

"Soon I'll have to call you Mr. President."

"Now *that* I'd let you call me."

As they walked away toward the trees, her mother said, "Dave?"

"Who's Dave?" her father said.

"Apparently, *you* are."

"What are you talking about?"

"You just told the owner to call you Dave."

"No, I didn't."

"Betsy," her mother said.

"You said Dave," Betsy said.

"I did *not.*"

"You absolutely did," Betsy said.

"You're messing with me."

"You've never been a Dave," her mother said.

"And I'm still not."

"You're the one who said it," Betsy said.

"Well, whoever Dave is," her father said, "I left him back in Iowa."

They walked up and down rows of trees looking for the best one left. They knew it when they saw it — a tall, fat tree with one small bald patch they could hide against the wall. Betsy and her mother held the tree while her father lay on the ground and worked the saw through the base of the trunk. It was slow going, back and forth with the blade, and Betsy could see her father's breath, and then she felt the weight of the tree and had to brace herself to steady it. Her mother liked to think she was stronger than she was. The tree almost fell on her. Betsy's father dropped the saw and jumped up to help.

It was only later, after sunset, the tree up but not yet decorated, that her mother noticed. Betsy could tell by her face that something was wrong. "Oh no," she said. "David." She was grabbing her left hand with her right as if maybe she had stuck herself with a hook.

"My ring," she said.

When Betsy was much younger, she'd been obsessed with her mother's ring, a platinum band with her parents' initials and their wedding date engraved on the inside.

She kept asking why her mother wore the ring, why her father had given it to her, what it meant to be married, could *she* marry her father someday, could she marry her mother. Betsy would ask to try it on, and her mother would let her, and every time she'd say, "It's so strange not to have it on my finger." Her mother wouldn't let Betsy wear it long and would never let it out of her sight.

She had lost weight, and it was cold, and her skin was probably dry, and it must have slipped off.

"Maybe it's in the car," her father said.

"I don't think I had it then."

"Let me check."

"It won't be there," her mother said, and then she left the room. She didn't cry often, but when she did, she didn't like anyone to see.

"If it isn't in the car, I'll drive back to the tree farm," her father said.

"But it's Christmas Eve," Betsy said.

"You two can decorate the tree without me."

As David left the house, he almost stepped on a bird. He saw it at the last moment, a large, obviously dead bird at the bottom of the stoop. Some kind of hawk, which didn't make sense on Delancey Place. What also didn't make sense, not that he was a bird expert, was that it didn't have any wounds. It didn't look as if a cat had mauled it. Its body was clean. You wouldn't know anything was wrong with it except that it was so still and its talons were clenched in a weird way. He'd seen a few dead birds before, but this was the biggest he'd ever seen.

David had a bad feeling about the bird. He remembered a client he'd had years earlier when he was practicing law. They were in his office, and a bird flew into the window, a loud thud that scared both of them out of their chairs. The man ran to the window.

"Thank God," the man said.

"For what?"

"It flew away," he said. "A dead bird is very bad."

"Bad for the bird."

"For us," the man said. "If a bird flies into your window and dies — very bad. If you find a dead bird on your property — also very bad."

David wasn't sure what to do with the bird. He didn't want to leave it there, but he also didn't want to touch it. He found a long stick by the curb and nudged the bird to make sure. It was stiff, and heavier than

David had imagined it would be. He got two bags and the snow shovel. He held his breath and shimmied the shovel under the bird, then with one hand lifted it while holding a trash bag open with the other. The bird didn't go in cleanly. David had to open the bag wider and reposition the bird on the shovel and push it in. Then he put the bag with the bird into the other bag, tied it, and put the bags into the trash can in the alley behind the house.

After an hour at the tree farm, David was sure he wasn't going to find the ring. The owner said he could keep looking, but it was Christmas Eve, just before closing, and it didn't seem right to keep him from his family. David spent fifteen more minutes taking baby steps around where he'd cut down the tree.

He thanked the owner and drove home. He scanned for Christmas music on the radio, and there was plenty, but the same songs he would have been happy to hear a few hours earlier now depressed him. So he turned off the radio.

When he arrived home, he told Danielle how sorry he was.

She said, "It's okay, you tried."

"I feel awful."

"Don't."

"Let me feel awful."

"David, it's all right."

He hugged her and kept telling her he was sorry; he wanted to say more.

"It's my fault anyway," she said.

"It's not your fault."

Which was what he'd said to her seven years earlier, after the accident.

FEBRUARY 1992

As soon as Betsy turned the corner, her stomach went nervous, but only when she took in the specifics — news vans blocking the street, lights and cameras in front of the house — did she make a connection between the commotion and her father.

It could have had something to do with Iowa, which he'd won four days earlier, or with New Hampshire, four days away, but somehow she understood that this could not have been about anything good.

Maybe he'd said something he shouldn't have, but to garner *this* kind of attention he would have had to say something truly terrible or stupid, and it wasn't like him to say terrible or stupid things, he was careful, he knew how to shut up and let others say terrible or stupid things, like how when they used to play Ping-Pong, Betsy and Nick versus Dad, he drove them crazy with his flawless defensive game, his laser focus on returning, not one attempt at a winner, until one of them, usually Betsy, made an unforced error. He was the same way during the campaign.

Betsy thought: Car accident, plane crash, assassination.

She walked faster, and as she got closer, about halfway down the street, she saw two cameramen laughing, maybe some crack one had made to the other, and she guessed that no one would be joking, not in front of their home, had her father been hurt.

It was bitter cold and windy and she hadn't worn gloves, and was carrying a bag, and her hands were freezing, and she really wanted to be home and warm. In the bag was a box, and in the box was a tie she'd bought for her father at Brooks Brothers — rather, a tie she'd bought to be from her mother to her father. She always bought him ties, they both did, always blue, for every occasion — birthday, Christmas, Father's Day, anniversary, winning Iowa. This one was for Valentine's Day.

She closed her eyes and waited, imagining that when she opened them, the cameras and reporters would be gone.

And then there it was — the light beneath her eyelids, and with it, the Nick-feeling.

She couldn't remember the last time she'd felt this. It never showed up when she expected it or looked for it. She had lain in bed on the night of the Iowa caucuses and closed her eyes and tried to connect with Nick, looked for that light she wasn't even sure was real, but she couldn't sense him.

She could feel him now, could feel something, and it told her to stay away. She opened her eyes: they were all still in front of the house. She walked around the block to the alley behind the house and snuck in through the back.

She found her mother hiding in the tub. Her mother was fully dressed — jeans, a light blue sweater, wool socks.

"Has Dad been hurt?"

Her mother shook her head no.

That was the beginning and end of their conversation. That was all Betsy wanted to know. As long as her father wasn't hurt, they could handle whatever this was about.

She could have turned on the TV, could have gotten in the tub with her mother and closed the curtain, could have snuck out the back of the house and taken her mother with her, but somehow she knew what to do and had the bravery to do it: she walked out the front door, still carrying the tie, and faced the cameras.

They charged the stoop. But, as if realizing it was just David Christie's daughter, not even old enough to vote, they paused.

But then one reporter asked her, and then they were all asking, what her reaction was to the news, the reports, the allegations, the photo, had she known, had her mother known, was it true, what did she know, how did she feel?

She knew to say nothing, what her father was so good at — let them talk and talk and make themselves look bad. She stood there stone-still. "Just a girl," she imagined someone might say. "Leave her alone. As if her mother having cancer isn't enough."

Betsy used the same tactic when her father came home that night. By then he had made three denials — in New Hampshire, upon his arrival in Philadelphia, and in front of his home — simple and quick.

Nothing but tabloid trash.

I love only my wife.

I'm determined to focus on the issues important to our country.

When he came inside, Betsy stared at him, and kept staring, until her father looked down.

And so without a word spoken between them, she knew.

■ ■ ■ ■

Danielle and Betsy sat on the couch. David sat on a chair across from them, leaning forward, elbows on his knees. He was wearing a dark gray suit but no tie.

He had been in politics too long by then, and the politician in him had spread like her cancer, Danielle thought. She didn't recognize him. He probably saw this moment — telling the truth to his wife and daughter — as one that could be spun, as if he were trying to maintain strong family favorables.

He said: *poor judgment, terrible mistake, foolish behavior.*

"Save that language for *them,*" Danielle said. "We're not *them.*"

David looked down like a boy ashamed.

She asked who, and he said, "Nobody," and she said, "Who *is* she?" and Betsy put her hands over her ears, and David said, "She's nobody," and for the first time Danielle raised her voice and said, "Everybody isn't standing in the cold outside our home because of *nobody.*"

"Please stop," Betsy said. "Please, please, please."

"I made a mistake," David said.

"David," Danielle said. She had an urge to repeat his name over and over as if to say: "David, it's *you.* Did you forget who you *are*?"

"David," she said again. She had no other words.

"Forget what's outside," he said. "Forget the campaign."

The phone rang. Betsy got up, walked calmly across the room, picked up the receiver, and then put it back into its cradle.

Immediately the phone rang again. She unplugged it, then left the room.

"So stupid," David said.

"I don't want to hear another word," Danielle said.

"So stupid."

"Stop," Danielle said. "I can't feel sorry for you."

Except she did. She wished she didn't, but she did. She knew what it was like to make a terrible mistake.

But four days later, when David finished third in New Hampshire, she no longer felt sorry, and five days after that, when he finished fifth in Maine, she didn't feel sorry, and the day after that, when he suspended his campaign, she didn't feel the least bit sorry, and now that the campaign was finally over — there would never be another campaign — she was ready to hear everything. The whole truth and nothing but. Every single thing that led to the photo of her husband with some woman straightening his tie in front of a hotel. They were going to sit down and he was going to tell her and they would be done with that part of it. The whole truth at once, like tearing off a bandage — the way Betsy had pulled off Danielle's bandage after the accident, when they had their election-night picnic on Franklin Field. One rip. Gone.

"How did it happen?"

"I'm not sure."

"No, tell me — how did you meet this person?"

"I was greeting a crowd before a speech."

"Where?"

"New York."

"When?"

"August."

"Before or after my diagnosis?"

"Before."

"And even after you knew — Christ, David, I feel sick."

"We don't have to do this."

"We do."

"We don't have to do it *now.*"

"We're not going anywhere. I'll get sick on this rug if I have to. So you were greeting your fans — go on."

"I was shaking hands, and all that, and this woman —"

"Her."

"Yes, she handed me a piece of paper, and I put it in my pocket."

"Why?"

"I don't know."

"Tell me."

"I don't *know*. If I could go back in time —"

"You can't."

"If."

"You can't."

"But if I *could,* I'd drop that paper, never look at it."

"Do you still have it?"

"Of course not."

"If I were to look through your pockets and your dresser and your files —"

"I don't have it."

"What was it — a love note? A proposition? What?"

"Her name, phone number."

"No note?"

"*I know you.* That was the whole note."

"Did you know her?"

"No."

"And you decided it was a good idea to call her."

"I thought maybe she did know me."

"That's not what you thought."

"I'm answering your questions, okay?"

"So you called her — then what?"

The truth was he had met her in the Algonquin Hotel lobby. He'd just finished meeting with potential donors and was about to leave for the airport when he saw her sitting alone at the hotel bar. It was a Friday around five o'clock. She looked familiar, but he couldn't recall her name or how he knew her. She had shoulder-length dark hair; her features were dark too — her eyes, her skin — and he guessed that she might be Italian or Spanish, and God it was bugging him — how did he know her?

A car was waiting in front of the hotel, but he walked over to her. She looked up at him and smiled as if she *did* know him. She had a gap between her two front teeth — like Lauren Hutton.

"We know each other, don't we?"

"Are you someone famous?" she said.

"No."

"You look like an actor from a soap opera I used to watch."

David laughed; he hadn't laughed that

hard in a long time.

"I'm David."

"Rae," she said.

"Rae what?"

"Bautista."

"You look like a Rae Bautista."

"Oh really. What does a Rae Bautista look like?"

"Like you."

"You look more like a Dave than a David."

"I've never been a Dave."

"You're totally a Dave," she said. "You should try being Dave for a while, see how it feels."

"So we really don't know each other?"

"We do now."

David's driver walked to the bar and said, "Sorry to interrupt, sir, but your flight." Then he went back outside.

"I *knew* you were famous," Rae said.

"Just because I have to catch a flight?"

"Okay, *sir.*"

"Are *you* famous?"

"Not yet," she said.

David shook her hand and said, "It was nice to meet you."

"We've already met — remember?"

"Right."

"Hey, maybe we knew each other in a past life."

"Maybe," David said.

"Or maybe we've already met in the future."

"Sounds like science fiction."

"Time isn't a straight line, Dave."

David realized that he was still holding her hand; he let go.

"I have to go," he said. "Good luck getting famous."

"I was joking about that," she said.

"Good," David said, "because I hear being famous sucks."

"Hold on," she said. She reached into her purse and took out a paperback book and a pen. She tore out a page from the book, then laid the book on the bar. David could see the title, *Bright Lights, Big City.* She wrote something on the page, folded it, and gave it to David. "See you in the next life," she said.

This was hardly the first note a woman had handed David. He always gave them to Tim Swisher. He put the note in his jacket pocket with the intention of doing the same. Then he went outside where his car was waiting.

He didn't look at the note until he was on his flight to Des Moines. Tim was sleeping in the seat next to him.

It said: *Now I know you.*

And her name. And her phone number.

"I didn't really know her," David said. "I'm not sure if that makes it better or worse."

"Nothing makes it better."

"I didn't love her."

"Then it was about sex."

"I don't know."

"David, come *on.*"

"I don't know what to say."

"She was *new,*" Danielle said.

"Yes."

"She wasn't *me.*"

"Like I told you, I didn't know her."

It was August and he was in his hotel room after two hours of doing what he hated most to do: asking for money. People he knew, people he didn't know, some people he didn't like. He had flown from Iowa to New York again just for this: to ask. To hold out his hand and say please. He wanted to *ask* over the phone — he hated that too — but Tim Swisher told him, "David, we're talking *very* deep pockets. These need to be face-to-face." He took off his jacket and tossed it onto the bed, and it landed in such a way that he could see its inside pocket.

Her number was in that pocket. In the two weeks since they had met, he had moved the note from jacket to jacket. He had read the two pages of *Bright Lights, Big City* three or four times, and kept telling himself: Give the note to Tim Swisher. Or just tear it into pieces and throw it away.

But now, back at the Algonquin, where he had met her, he took out the note, unfolded it, and looked at her name. He had the strangest sense that he had known this name for a very long time. He imagined that she was still sitting downstairs in the hotel bar. Her number had a 718 area code. He picked up the phone and dialed.

Their conversation was brief: he invited her to his room; she said she could be there in a half hour. She didn't ask why he wanted to see her — she must have known by then who he was — and he didn't offer a reason.

"Come straight to the room and knock once."

"Whatever you say."

"Straight to the room — do you understand?"

"Yes, Dave."

That name, and the way she said it, stirred something in him, and by the time he heard her single knock thirty minutes later, he had almost convinced himself that there was David Christie and there was another man named Dave, whose existence might begin and end in this room.

She was wearing a red skirt and red heels.

After hello, but before either said anything else, she kicked off her heels and stood there barefoot, three inches shorter, but still tall. He sat on the bed and looked at her. She opened her mouth slightly, and he saw the gap between her front teeth. He loosened his blue tie and unbuttoned the top button.

She put her thumb against her lips, then moved the tip of her thumb into her mouth.

He stood, moved closer.

She didn't move back, and now they were close enough to touch. She put one bare foot on top of the other, and then he reached out for her, replaced her thumb with his own.

She would leave notes in David's ticket pocket. Always the same pocket, never anywhere else. Republicans made a stink over the fact that David's suits *had* ticket pockets — a sign of his East Coast elitism, they said, despite the fact that he grew up middle class. The notes were risky, but she signed them *T.* or *T. S.* so that anyone who saw them would think they were from Tim Swisher. David would wait until he was on the plane to Iowa or Florida or wherever he was holding babies that week. *Pleased with the way things went down. You performed well, really connected. Keep it up. Plenty more low-hanging fruit to look forward to.* He'd read the note a few more times at the hotel. Then, guilty after a call with Danielle, he would tear the note into pieces so tiny that no one, not even the most ambitious tabloid journalist, would be able to reconstruct it.

She had girly handwriting. Large, curvy letters, bubbles over her *i*'s. To be safe, she would write small and sloppy, but not so sloppy that David wouldn't be able to read her words. She told him that she hated having to write *David* or *Senator* rather than *Dave*. Once, he held her note up to a light and could see that she had written *xoxo* but then erased it. At first David refused to give her notes, but she was hurt. She was good at being hurt. She cried; she spoke like a child. Sometimes, she sucked her thumb in her sleep. David felt sorry for her; he gave in. He wrote letters, but only with his left hand and never addressed to her. He signed off *Thanks* or *Thanks for your help* or *Take care* or *Best wishes* or *All the best* or *Best.*

She wanted *Love,* but David said no way. She wanted *xoxo.* No way. She wanted *Fondly* or *Warmly,* but he said no, too risky.

"Come on, it's *me*," she said, as if David had known her his entire life and not just a few months.

She said, "It's not like I'm going to the *Enquirer*."

"Did you use protection?"

"No."

"David, you put me at risk."

"She was tested."

"Tested for *what*?"

"She was tested, okay?"

"How do *you* know? Because she told you?"

David closed his eyes and moved his lips as if practicing what he could possibly say.

"She could be pregnant," Danielle said.

"She's not."

"So you pulled out every time."

"No."

"So she could be."

"She was on the pill."

"And you believed her — this woman you didn't know."

"I saw her take it."

"So what?"

"So she's not."

"Not what?"

David hesitated.

"Say it," Danielle said.

"She's not — pregnant."

"If I have to say *pulled out* — for God's sake, you have to say that."

It ended in early February at the Algonquin, where it began. David had not seen Rae since December. When he told her it was over, she cried but stayed calm. She stood beside the bed, but he would not move any closer to her, would not comfort her. She already knew, she told him. She knew when she called his hotel suite in Des Moines the week before Christmas and he canceled their plan for her to fly to Iowa. The businesslike way he had spoken to her, his tone of voice — she knew.

"I have a family," he said now.

"I'm well aware," she said.

"We made a mistake."

She walked over to him and stood too close; he looked away from her. "Sometimes," she said, "we make mistakes for a reason."

"I'm sorry for my part in this," he said.

"Mistakes were made," she said. "Isn't that what you're supposed to say?"

"I have to go," David said.

She hugged him and, with her arms wrapped tightly around him, she said that everything happens for a reason and maybe

153

he did need to walk away from her — for now — because that would give him the space and clarity so that at some point — she *knew* this, she told him — the two of them could be together more "cleanly."

David didn't disagree with her — not verbally. He didn't want to do anything to set her off. He told her again that he was sorry.

"Don't be," she said.

She reached into her bag, pulled out a box, and gave it to David. "This is *not* a good-bye gift," she said.

David opened the box; it was a dark blue tie with white stripes. She said she'd bought it at Barney's before Christmas. He thanked her and put the tie into his bag.

"I want you to wear it," she said.

"I will."

"Now," she said. "Please," she added in baby talk. She pouted her lips, trying to look sad, David assumed, but it looked more like she was blowing a kiss. He could easily get pulled back in, he knew that.

"I have a flight to catch."

Iowa is a week away, he thought. New Hampshire is eight days after that.

"If this is the last time we're ever going to see each other," she said, "if you really mean that, then please just let me see you in the tie."

David, wanting this to be over before it could start again, quickly pulled off the tie he was wearing — Betsy had given it to him for Christmas — and replaced it with the tie Rae had given him.

He walked to the door with his bag. "I really need to go."

Rae didn't move from where she stood.

"You need to go first," David said.

Rae asked if they could walk out together. He said no. So she bargained: okay, she understood why they couldn't leave his room together, but just once couldn't they leave the hotel together? No, he said, much too risky. Okay, she said, but how about together but not together, like two strangers who happened to be leaving at the same time, and he hesitated, and she rubbed her eyes, perhaps to remind him that she had been crying, and said please, and then put the tip of her thumb into her mouth and waited, and he said, "Two strangers."

Down in the lobby, David walked through the revolving door first, Rae behind him. Outside, they stood in front of the hotel — two strangers, it would seem.

She'll walk away, he thought, and I'll wait here for a car to bring me to the airport, and time will pass, and eventually it will be as if this never happened.

But then she walked closer to him and said, "Aren't you Dave Christie?"

He wasn't sure what she was up to. Maybe she was trying to start over as if they'd never met.

Sorry, he thought, but Dave is dead.

And then: She's dangerous.

"I just wanted to ask for your autograph," she said.

She handed him an Algonquin notepad and pen.

As he was signing his name, she touched him. "Your tie's crooked. Who dressed you today?" She smiled, but he didn't return it.

She centered the tie, and then tightened the knot around his collar — too tight, he felt.

"Better," she said, and when he said nothing in reply, she touched his face and said, "Bye — for now."

She walked away. David stood there holding the pen and his own autograph. He dropped both in the trash in front of the hotel. He watched her walking slowly — too slowly — down the street. She stopped, and he was worried that she might turn around. But she started walking again. He was relieved when she turned a corner and he could no longer see her.

MARCH 2, 1992

When Nick died, Betsy had wanted to return to school right away, though she came to see that as a mistake. Now, she never wanted to go back. She was a senior in high school, she had sent in her college applications, but she had missed two weeks of school, and it wasn't like anyone had died this time. The principal had been very understanding; everyone had. "Take as much time as you need," her teachers said. Some offered to meet with her one-on-one. But two weeks was probably enough, she decided. The longer her absence, the more attention she would receive upon her return. Maybe everyone was talking about her. Or maybe no one really cared.

If asked how she was doing, what would she say?

Fine, thanks.

Good, how are you?

Hanging in there.

It hasn't been easy.

To be honest, life kind of sucks.

The truest answer might be to say nothing. Because she really didn't have the words. Maybe she did, but it would be too complicated, too much for polite conversation.

She would have to explain that as bad as it was to hear her parents fighting — sometimes in the middle of the night — worse was to hear their silence, and worst was to be barely able to hear them, to know that they were trying to keep their voices down for her benefit.

Some nights she couldn't hear everything they said, only words, phrases.

I feel sick.

Love note.

It was about sex.

Bullshit.

Pulled out.

Pregnant.

She lay awake in bed now and could hear them. Their bedroom was at the other end of the hallway, Nick's old room between them, and their voices were low. It was after midnight: already Monday, the day she had decided to return to school. She was too nervous to sleep. That her parents were

159

awake and talking at this time usually didn't mean something good. She reached in the dark to her bedside table and turned on her shortwave radio. She turned the dial, English, English, Spanish, English, German, until she heard a language she didn't know: it sounded Arabic. But the man's voice was too loud, he sounded upset, and so she kept turning until she found a woman speaking French. Her voice was like a song. Betsy brought the radio into bed and rested it against her ear, and it was as if this woman were in the room with her. Her parents' voices faded.

Just as she was about to fall asleep, the radio went silent. She turned the dial, but there was nothing; the batteries had gone dead. There were new batteries downstairs in a kitchen drawer, but she didn't want to get up and walk past her parents' room. Their voices went up and down in waves. Then she thought she heard — yes, she did — her mother crying. Betsy got out of bed and went to her door; she opened it a crack and listened. She remembered how frightened she'd been the first time she heard her mother cry. Betsy was seven, and her mother had banged her knee on the bottom of the dining room table, and the pain brought tears to her eyes, and then Betsy started to cry, and hugged her mother and said, "Stop, please stop, please." Before that, she hadn't understood that adults cried.

She had an urge to do something similar now — to walk down the hallway and into her parents' room without knocking, and say, "Stop, please stop."

She wanted to shake them and say, "Look at me — it's Betsy, your daughter. Look at each other. It's *you*. It's *us*. We're okay, we're going to be okay. No one died."

But she couldn't decide whether that would help or hurt. She was having trouble making any sort of decision lately. She had decided to return to school, that was something, but now she stood in her bedroom doorway and could not decide what to do — which itself was a kind of decision. She waited and listened and stayed where she was.

Now fully awake and feeling alone, she reached to turn on the shortwave, then remembered that the batteries were dead.

She didn't watch much TV, especially not this late, but she turned it on. The theme song of *M*A*S*H* depressed her. She had only ever seen the show in reruns, and the music, now, reminded her of a time before she was born. She changed the channel. A late-night comedian was telling jokes, and it was nice to hear actual people laugh rather than a laugh track. The comedian, a tall man with dark wavy hair and a Brooklyn accent, was talking about how his wife was always mad at him — he used too much toilet paper, he snored, he was a slob, he didn't make enough money — but now, finally, he had the perfect response: "Hey, at least I'm not David Christie." The audience laughed, and Betsy was too stunned to turn the channel. The comedian went on: "Did you hear what David Christie said now? Did you hear what this guy said? He said about his mistress, 'I don't love her.' " After a pause: "Real smart, man, now you've got *two* women mad at you. Great, way to go." Now the audience's reaction did sound like a laugh track. Betsy wanted to turn off the TV, but didn't. She kept listening. "This guy, I'm telling you, he makes a terrible husband like me look pretty good. You remember during his campaign, he was always talking about how there are two Americas. Well, no wonder: in one America he was faithful to his wife, and in the other America he was, in fact, banging his mistress."

Enough.

Betsy turned off the TV, got back into bed, closed her eyes, and listened: the house was quiet. She thought about Nick, mental snapshots of him at different ages, each for only a few seconds before it was replaced by a new one, and suddenly he was sixteen, and there was nowhere to go but back in time: her brother got younger and younger until he was the youngest she remembered him, when she was three and he was nine. She shut her eyes more tightly and could see in the darkness beneath her eyelids strange shapes and flashes of light, and she looked for her brother in them. She'd seen him there before, but never when she tried; he showed up, if it was him, on his own terms. She tried to have Nick be the last thing she thought of before falling asleep, hoping she might dream about him, but when she woke in the morning, she couldn't remember any dreams at all.

She showed up to her first class early and asked her English teacher if she might change her seat. She wanted to sit near the door, if that was okay, and her teacher said, "Of course." The idea behind this request was that if she wanted to leave, if she needed to, she would be only a few feet from the door, and she could be gone without having to see anyone's reaction.

But as the other students started arriving

to class and took their seats behind her —
Betsy kept her head down, pretending to
look through her bag for something — she
realized that she had made a mistake: she
had asked to sit where everyone could see
her. And so before all the seats were taken,
Betsy went up to her teacher and said, "I'm
sorry, but I changed my mind. Is it okay if I
sit in the last row instead?"

"Sure, whatever you need," her teacher
said.

But this too turned out not to be the best
decision, Betsy realized, as she now had to
pack up her books, with everyone watching,
and walk to the back of the class — looking
down, not meeting anyone's eyes — and call
even more attention to herself than had she
simply stayed in the front or, even better,
never asked to change her assigned seat in
the first place. Some of her friends turned
to look at her; one even mouthed, "I'm so
sorry." She could have used their support,
but she was embarrassed and didn't want to
hear their sympathy, genuine though it
would be.

Later, she asked if she could skip lunch —
not skip eating, she didn't mean that, she
explained, but eat somewhere alone, maybe
in a classroom.

Whatever you need.

That's what everyone was going to say to any request she made, it seemed. The kind of thing you'd say to someone who had experienced a death in the family.

She wanted to say: "No one died!"

Except she did feel that someone or something had.

After lunch, upon remembering that comedian's jokes, she made another decision. It came to her suddenly and clearly, and even though she hadn't made the best decisions today, she knew that this decision was right. She went straight to her guidance counselor and told him: she'd changed her mind about colleges. She'd applied only to schools on the East Coast — Columbia, Penn, Amherst, Swarthmore, Bowdoin — but she realized now that she might want to go farther away, maybe Stanford or UCLA or Pomona. Her guidance counselor, Mr. Alford, a thin man who always wore white shirts and bow ties and had glasses and a graying goatee, asked if she was sure, and she said yes, and then he said, "So, do you mean you'd apply next year? Because all the deadlines have passed."

"I was hoping maybe they could make an exception," she said. "Maybe you could talk to someone."

"I'd be glad to reach out to them," Mr.

Alford said, "but I'm not sure if they'd even be allowed to make an exception."

He must have seen the disappointment on Betsy's face, and of course he had to know that this was her first day back. "I'll try," he said. "I'll do whatever I can."

But in AP Calculus at the end of the day, Betsy's mind wandered back to Mr. Alford. She imagined the conversations he might have with directors of admissions at the schools Betsy had mentioned.

Yes, that Christie.

His daughter.

She's going through a tough time.

One of our best students.

I know, but under the circumstances.

Before she left school for home, she went to see Mr. Alford. But as she waited outside his office for him, she decided that she didn't want to talk to him after all; she just wanted to leave. So she left him a note:

Dear Mr. Alford,

Thank you so much for being willing to help me, but I'm really not sure, and I think I should stick with the schools I applied to. I'll probably defer anyway.

Thank you again.

Betsy

No, she couldn't make up her mind about much these days. Should she eat two cookies or stop at one? Should she glance at tabloid covers in the supermarket or look away? Should she sneak into Nick's room at night and sleep in his bed? Should she suggest that her parents sleep there? Should she ever turn on her TV again? Should she write a letter to that comedian? Should she write an editorial, or something? She could call it "Please Leave Us Alone" or "People Make Mistakes" or "This Is Not Funny" or "My Parents Love Each Other, Really They Do, I Swear."

But the worst were those moments when she couldn't make up her mind about the one thing she used to be certain about: Did her parents really love each other? They seemed to love each other; she wanted to believe that they did. But was love about feeling or action? If you felt love for someone but did not act so, could you really say that you loved that person? Or was true love when you acted loving toward someone even when you did not feel it — and who felt it all the time anyway? Or could you love someone — maybe this was what she believed — but act beneath that love? And if you acted beneath that love often enough, very far beneath it, could you kill it?

167

When she got home from school, her mother was sleeping and her father had closed himself up in his office down the hall. She went to her own room, and so they were all alone together.

MARCH 15, 1992

One Sunday morning, a month after the story broke, cold enough to remind Betsy that winter wasn't over but sunny enough and with enough birdsong to remind her that spring was a week away, she believed that everything would be okay. Maybe her father did too. Her mother's cancer was neither spreading nor remitting, the press wasn't feeding on them with quite the same frenzy, the nomination process had carried on without her father, and Betsy hoped they'd be okay.

The night before, for the first time in a month, her parents had slept in the same bed. Her father got up early, like when she and Nick were kids, to make pancakes. Betsy smelled them in her sleep and woke convinced that she was a child again and Nick was in his room down the hall.

She found her father in plaid pajamas,

pouring batter. With his back to her he could have been a younger man, but when he turned and smiled, she could see how much the campaign and the past month had aged him. There were more lines around his eyes, and his hair had more gray.

Her mother came down and made coffee. Betsy thought she was seeing things when her mother pressed her face into her father's back and wrapped her arms around him. He closed his eyes. The batter in the pan started to bubble, but she didn't want her parents to move. As quietly as possible she took the spatula from her father's hand and flipped the pancake.

After breakfast she had the idea that they might drive to Valley Forge and walk the trails as they'd done almost every Sunday when she and Nick were kids. Even though her mother wasn't strong enough to walk nearly as far as they used to, she loved the idea, and of course her father did. They didn't bother to clean up their mess — the kitchen counter was splattered with batter and syrup — and within ten minutes they were dressed and in the car.

Her father opened the window and wind blew his hair wild, and this made her mother laugh. He hadn't shaved in a week. He'd gotten dressed in such a rush, almost as if Betsy's mother might change her mind, that he'd put on two different socks, one black and one gray. He was just some absentminded dad driving his family to the park, Betsy thought, and the rest of it — speeches and fundraisers and press conferences and debates — was over. None of it had ever happened. Except Nick, that is. Nothing could change that the other side of the back seat was empty.

The realization that Nick was still gone was the first blip in Betsy's blissful morning. The second was the sudden change in her mother's demeanor. At first she seemed to be wincing from cancer pain — that sometimes happened — but then Betsy saw that her mother was mumbling to herself — something angry. Her father looked at her mother, then turned back to face the road.

Her mother was getting louder. She closed her eyes and shook her head. "No. No. No," she said, as if trying to make some truth go away. Then, as they drove through the park, her mother opened the car door and tried to jump out.

Her father grabbed her mother's shoulder. From behind, Betsy pulled her mother's coat to hold her back. But she fought like a wounded, trapped animal and pushed herself out of the car just as it came to a stop.

Her mother fell but got up, then ran across the road and into a vast field. She paused only to take off her coat and sweater and let them fall to the grass. She kept running. Whitetail deer feeding on the tips of bush branches hopped away to the farthest borders of the field, where they stopped and turned to stare.

They ran after her, the car idling in the road. The farther her mother ran into the field, the taller the grass. Her legs must have been too tired to keep going. She fell.

They couldn't see her, but found her by her sobs.

Her father sat on the ground beside her mother, then lay upon her. Betsy's mother made herself small and pulled at the neckline of her blouse as if it were choking her, and her father held her mother and covered her until all Betsy could see was him. *He* seemed to be the one sobbing, but her mother was crying beneath him, and Betsy had never loved her parents more, had never been more frightened and hopeful, or felt as sorry for all of them as she did now.

They helped her mother back to the car. She sat in the back seat with Betsy, where Nick used to sit.

When they arrived home, her father got into bed with her mother. He didn't bother to take off his boots. Betsy wanted to stay there and watch them. She wanted the story to end there. But there was still the mess to clean up. So she went to the kitchen and scrubbed the breakfast plates. She wiped batter from the stove. She soaked the pan, then washed and dried it.

Only later, toward dusk, did she notice the butter and milk, which she'd left out. It was too late. The butter had melted. The milk had gone bad. Her parents didn't get up for dinner. At some point during the night, frightened, Betsy got into bed with them.

Early the next morning, the phone rang and rang, but they didn't answer.

■ ■ ■ ■

PART FOUR:
CONCEDE

2010

■ ■ ■ ■

MARCH 15, 2010

"I think you have a crush on Ford," Peter Swann says.

"Better than yours on Dukakis," Avery says.

"I've always dreamed of riding in a tank."

This was Peter's idea: to pretend that their Presidential Politics paper is due tomorrow when really it's due the day *after* tomorrow. He pulls all-nighters to write papers, but always a night early. He suggested to Avery that they might work better together, run ideas by each other, keep each other awake, whatever, and this sounded good to Avery, not the no-sleep part — she rarely stays up past midnight — but the part about hanging out with Peter, sharing ideas, and especially *whatever*. In the month since they practice-kissed on Valentine's Day, they have for-real kissed, and engaged in some minor *whatever*, mostly standing up. When

177

she's barefoot, her lips line up with his chin; when she rises up on her toes, it's just right. So far, tonight, they've worked, Avery at her desk, Peter at her roommate's desk. Avery's roommate, a first-year who doesn't know that her relationship with her high school boyfriend, to whom she's secretly engaged, is doomed — as are almost all relationships that predate college — is visiting him again at Bucknell. She's gone so often that Avery practically has a single.

Peter abandons his desk and lies across Avery's bed widthwise, his feet touching the floor.

"Ford's real name, you know, was Leslie Lynch King Jr."

"No wonder he changed it," Peter says.

"Doesn't roll off the tongue like Peter Swann."

"Or Avery Modern."

"We'd make a great ticket — at least in name. Swann Modern."

"Modern Swann," Peter says. "You can be on top."

Avery closes her laptop and lies next to Peter, her feet beside his on the floor. "So we've moved on to the flirtation stage of the all-nighter."

"Politics and flirtation," Peter says. "They go hand in hand."

Avery rolls onto her side, puts one leg between Peter's; he turns to face her.

"Read my lips," Peter says, and then he kisses Avery. His glasses are in the way, so she takes them off and tosses them behind her on the bed. She likes the feel of his stubble, likes to put her hands in his hair, which is dark and loosely curled. He touches her lips with his thumb, and they pull back to look at each other. Without his glasses he could be a different person: his eyes seem bluer, his eyelashes longer.

"Who knew," he says. "Gerald Ford as aphrodisiac."

"Actually," she says, "you need to see the photo of him all muscular and handsome in his Michigan football uniform."

"You really do have a crush on President Bumbler."

"You see, that's just it," she says. "You think of Ford, you see him stumbling down the steps coming off Air Force One or trying to eat a shuck-wrapped tamale."

"That's *not* what cost him the '76 election."

"In this country," Avery says, "it might have."

"Never should have pardoned Nixon."

"So people should never be pardoned?"

"Are you a closeted Republican?"

"Seriously," Avery says, "this guy's father — his biological father — threatened to kill him and his mother with a butcher knife. His parents separated when he was only two weeks old. He didn't even know about his father until he was seventeen. He won two national football championships at Michigan, passed up contract offers from the Lions and Packers to coach boxing — *boxing* — at Yale, where he eventually got his law degree. He enlisted in the navy after Pearl Harbor. And all anyone thinks of when they think of Gerald Ford is Chevy Chase blowing his nose into his tie, pouring a glass of water into his ear, and falling on his head."

Peter says, "I think you just wrote your paper."

"And listen — I bet you don't know this, no one ever talks about this — two assassination attempts — *two* — seventeen days apart, both by women."

"You're blowing my mind," Peter says. "And kind of turning me on."

"He was a fucking Eagle Scout, man."

Peter laughs. "Okay, now you're making shit up."

"Don't get me started on Kennedy."

"Was he an Eagle Scout too?"

"Shit no," Avery says. "And that's the

point of my paper. The *image* of Kennedy was this *GQ*-Polo-Ivy-preppy-athletic guy on his sailboat, but really his spine was so messed up he could hardly walk. Meanwhile Ford was probably the most athletic president ever, and yet the *image* of him is Chevy fucking Chase."

"So I take it you're not a fan of *Caddyshack.*"

"Never seen it," Avery says.

"I may need a new running mate," Peter says. "Who vetted you?"

"At least I'm not defending a guy in a helmet who rode around in a tank with a stupid grin on his face."

"I'm not defending him," Peter says. "The assignment was to analyze — objectively analyze — an image from presidential politics."

"Okay, but is there any heart in your paper?"

"I'm calling it 'Tanked.' "

"No heart."

"Should there be?"

"Yes."

"Well, maybe you heart Ford more than I heart Dukakis."

Peter rolls on top of Avery and kisses her. With one hand she touches his face and with the other she reaches around him and grabs the back of his belt, pulls his weight down onto her.

What it feels like, Betsy decides, is popcorn popping in her stomach. She hates popcorn, the smell when Cal pops it, the unpopped kernels at the bottom of the blue bowl he always uses. She's warm in bed and doesn't want to get up, but she's going to be sick, just the thought of popcorn is enough, worse to imagine kernels popping in her belly. She tries to take deep breaths. Lately she's found herself needing deep breaths. Sometimes this works, sometimes it makes her feel worse. Her breathing's now quick and shallow, and she starts to hyperventilate, a wonky light-headed feeling that makes her lips tingle. The covers are too heavy; she throws them off. She closes her eyes in the dark and her hands and feet are tingling too and soon she will float away. That wouldn't be so bad, she thinks.

Eight weeks and she isn't showing. She knows soon that will change. On their wedding day in September she'll be eight months pregnant.

Cal wakes. He used to be a deep sleeper, but now, even asleep, he can detect her slightest discomfort.

"What's wrong?"

"Nothing."

"Are you sure?"

"Do you think I'm lying?"

"I'm just asking."

Betsy turns away from him and stares at the bedroom window. She tries to follow a drop of rain rolling down the glass. Then another.

Cal rubs her back. She's mad at him for not being mad at her; he should be.

"Maybe we should move."

"Bets, we just moved here four months ago."

"Forget it."

"You do that a lot, you know."

"Do what?"

"Say something, then say forget it."

"Okay, let's try again," she says. "Maybe we should move."

"You wanted to move back home."

"You agreed it was a good idea."

"Because it was what *you* wanted," he says. "I wouldn't have chosen to leave my clients, move here, and find new ones."

"Forget it."

"You just did it again."

"You're always asking what's wrong."

"Would you like me to stop asking?"

"Yes."

"Fine."

"Forget it — you can keep asking."

"You just —"

"I did it again, I know."

"I'm not even awake," Cal says.

"Sorry I woke you."

"Stop saying you're sorry."

"Stop asking what's wrong."

"I already said I would."

"Nothing's wrong," Betsy says.

"Okay, nothing's wrong."

"I want you to believe me."

"You want me to believe you."

"Stop repeating what I say."

"I'm just validating your feelings."

"I'm not one of your patients."

"Clients."

"Let's try one more time," Betsy says. "Maybe we should move."

"Where?"

"Back to New York."

"You wanted to leave New York."

"I didn't *want* to."

"You needed a break."

"Yes."

"And now you're ready to go back."

"Maybe we should move to the middle of nowhere."

Cal sighs. "Is this about your father?"

"Yes, Dr. Westfall. How astute of you."

"We're engaged. I'm allowed to ask a

fucking question."

There — finally. Some anger.

"I'm sorry," Betsy says.

"Me too."

"You didn't do anything wrong."

"Well, I'm sorry anyway."

"Let *me* be sorry."

"Apology accepted."

Cal puts his arm around her, lays his hand on her belly. She moves his hand up, presses it against her chest.

Her breathing changes, her body relaxes.

She pulls the covers over them.

She leans over David, this woman he almost recognizes. Maybe she's my wife, he thinks. Someone he's in a relationship with. Sleeping with. Her name he remembers: Tiffany. A name that makes him think of things airy, fragile. She smells like her name. She turns on the lamp beside his bed and he sees her body more clearly: pear-shaped, thick legs. The kind of curvy body he's always secretly liked. Full lips, the delicate hands of a smaller woman. Short blonde hair.

But if she's my wife, David thinks, why then did she just walk into my room from some other room? Why is she wearing light blue scrubs? Why the urge to ask her for help? Why the faint memory of having asked her for help many times? Help tying my shoelaces, pulling up my socks, buttoning my shirt, buckling my belt, getting in and out of bed. Why is a wheelchair at the foot of the bed?

She sets the chair's brake, sits David up, pulls him to the edge of the bed. Hugging David, her face against his chest, she lifts him into the chair. She releases the brake and pushes the chair to the bathroom. She parks the chair beside the toilet, sets the brake, pulls down his pajama bottoms. Bending at the knees, her arms around him, in one fluid motion she jerks his body up out of the chair and onto the toilet.

His bladder empties in starts and stops, and then Tiffany does everything she just did, but in reverse — lifts him from the toilet onto the chair, wheels him back to bed, lifts him from the chair onto the mattress.

He stares up into her face. "I'm sorry for asking," he whispers, "but are you my wife?"

"My name is Tiffany," she says.

"I know," he says, "but are you my wife?"

She points to a framed photograph on the dresser. "That was your wife."

The young man in the photo must be me, he thinks. With him and his wife are a boy, maybe in high school, and a younger girl.

"Are those my children?"

"Yes," she says.

"I'm happy to have children," he says, "but don't let them see me this way."

"I'm sure they'd want to see you, Mr. Christie."

"Don't let them, please," he says. "Not until I'm on my feet again."

Avery wakes in predawn darkness, her body heavy against the mattress, wind blowing rain against her window. She extends her arms and legs as if making a snow angel, a heavenly stretch, and realizes, with disappointment, that she's alone. She tries to slow down last night in her memory, but it returns to her in dreamlike flashes.

And then she hears a chair move. This startles her at first, just a little, until she hears typing — Peter on his laptop at her desk. She closes her eyes and listens to the rain and the typing. As much as she would like to say, "Good morning," or "Hey you," she worries that saying anything, or letting Peter know she's awake, would end this moment she doesn't want to end. Not even Peter in bed beside her, she thinks, could be better. The cold rain blowing outside makes her feel that much warmer, and she doesn't have to be in class until eleven, and she wants to remain in this heavy yet somehow weightless state — her body sinking into the bed — for as long as possible. She's comforted by the sound of someone awake while she almost-sleeps. When she was young, she liked knowing that her mother was up, liked hearing her footsteps downstairs, voices from the TV, ice cubes in a glass, her mother making herself a drink, some nights a tea kettle whistling, hot water poured into a mug, a spoon stirring honey, her mother on the phone with an old friend she used to go to auditions with.

Her active, hyper-analytical mind wants to convince her that it's weird for the boy she just had sex with to remind her of her mother, or that by feeling so safe with Peter in the room, she's placing too much importance on their relationship too soon and therefore making herself vulnerable, but the truth is, she had forgotten entirely about the comforting sounds of her mother awake at night, and only by feeling something similar with Peter was she able to retrieve those memories; otherwise, who knows, they might have been lost forever, hidden beneath more complicated memories: her mother as needy, childlike, messy.

Now he *is* gone.

Her eyes are open, and she can see the empty chair at her desk. Must be eight or nine, hard to tell: it's pouring, the sky so dark it could be dusk, as if she slept through the day.

She should check the time on her phone, which is on her desk, she should make sure, but as soon as she gets up, it will feel like a new day, whereas as long as she stays in bed, last night, in a way, can continue. The sheets smell like her and Peter — like sex. She moves her head to the pillow Peter used and tries to smell him. She feels silly, vulnerable, and stops; this is something her mother might do, probably did do. But when she brings her hand to her mouth to cover a yawn, she does smell Peter. She doesn't know what the smell is at first except that it's him and must be from when he was on top of her, holding her down by her hands. After, they joked that he had reversed the ticket — after all, she was supposed to be on top — and then this became shorthand for a move either could use: reversing the ticket. They didn't use protection, neither wanted to, they agreed he would pull out, but when the moment came and he started to, she wrapped her legs around him and held him inside, just for a few seconds longer, and then he pulled out just in time.

"I'm sorry about that," she told Peter, and he said, "Believe me, I didn't want to stop either," and she said, "I'm normally more responsible than that," and he said, "Next time, we'll be more careful." But as nice as she feels now, remembering last night, she also feels shaken that she almost did something so foolish — again, she thinks of her mother — and the *last* thing she wants is —

Pencils.

The smell on her hands.

Peter takes notes with pencils. He has a thing for *good* pencils, beautiful pencils from Japan and Germany and France that cost two dollars each, and sometimes vintage American pencils, and Avery gives him shit for it even though she finds it endearing, it's not some pose, he doesn't go around telling people — in fact, he asked her *not* to tell anyone. She said don't worry, she wouldn't tell the tabloids, and then she got quiet, and he asked what was wrong, and she pretended that nothing was and went back to ribbing him. He even carries around a two-hole KUM magnesium wedge sharpener, made in Germany, one hole for standard pencils, the other for giant pencils. They double-entendre'd the hell out of that — its extra-hard, tempered, high-carbon-steel blades, its optimum cutting angles, the precision molding of its inner parts. He uses each pencil until there's nothing left but the ferrule and eraser, and then he keeps the nubs in a glass jar on his desk.

That is the smell — graphite and cedar on his hands, now on hers.

Twenty minutes later, afraid she might miss class, she gets up to check the time. On her desk, beside her phone, is one of Peter's favorite pencils, a black Calepino no. 2 with white eraser, laid atop a folded piece of paper. The note reads:

Dear Avery Modern,
I'm watching you sleep. You are such a still sleeper.
    Thanks for the all-nighter. You inspire me.
        xo Peter Swann (aka Jerry Ford)

The day, the long day ahead, frightens Betsy. It's 10:30 AM and she's alone, tired, nauseous; she doesn't know what to do. She's always known what to do: stay busy, work hard, get things done. But today? Plan for the wedding? Read baby books? Get healthy — whatever that means? Since the move back to Philadelphia in November, she has continued to work remotely. Just enough to feel as though she has a purpose.

But the interim director seems to be doing well, and some days Betsy feels that she needs the foundation more than it needs her. She was the one who started it and grew it. She was the one who named it the Danielle Glass Foundation, as her mother had wished. Betsy suspected that this would hurt her father, and her mother had expressed her preference verbally, not in writing, so Betsy could have named it the Danielle Christie Foundation. No one would have known the truth. But she wanted to honor her mother's wish — funny, she thought at the time, how the feelings of the dead often trump those of the living — and maybe she did want to hurt her father, just a little, wanted her mother to get in the last jab. No matter, her father said he liked the name, liked to think of Danielle Glass, the young woman he fell in love with in college.

In twelve years the foundation has helped hundreds of high school students from economically depressed communities become first-generation college students. Betsy's mother had been the first in her family to attend college. Betsy knew how to recruit people — teachers, camp counselors, guidance counselors, therapists like Cal — and how to raise money, and how to publicize the foundation's work. The foundation was her baby, and there were always things to do.

But today she's scared: she can't think of what to *do*. Except sleep. If she sleeps, then at least she won't be able to think. The problem is, she's too anxious to sleep. She could go somewhere, get out, take a walk, but it's pouring, sheets of rain windblown against the window.

She walks around the house. She's been living here four months after not having lived here since she was eighteen, half her lifetime ago. She's confused by the rooms. Maybe it's from being so tired lately, her brain not as sharp, but as she moves from room to room, she isn't sure she knows what year it is or how old she is. She imagines for a moment that the past two decades have been a dream. Longer than that. None of it ever happened; they might try again. These rooms, to varying degrees, contain the past: her father's desk, his old Rolodex, his robe still in the closet, her mother's snow boots, too big for Betsy, a shelf of her mother's books, a bottle of her mother's perfume, one of Nick's football jerseys hanging in the attic. Too much of the present — Betsy's things, mostly — remains unpacked: boxes in the corner of the bedroom, in the basement, in otherwise empty rooms on the third floor. She and Cal sublet their apartment in Brooklyn for the year with no plan one way or another after that. Betsy sits on the lone chair in a room on the third floor, surrounded by boxes, and thinks: The wedding is six months away, a baby will be born a month later, and it would be so nice — Betsy wasn't kidding when she brought up the possibility with Cal this morning — to move somewhere very far away.

Very Far Away, a book by Maurice Sendak, is in one of these boxes, Betsy realizes. Betsy has never been a braggart, but she did tell her school friends that Maurice Sendak was her neighbor, a claim that wasn't exactly true. But the Rosenbach Museum and Library, which held much of Sendak's work — sketches, original artwork, first editions — *was* her neighbor. Two doors down. She would fall asleep some nights, especially that first year without Nick, and imagine that Sendak and Max from *Where the Wild Things Are* were close by, and if not for the house between them, Betsy might have called out, "Mr. Sendak, are you awake?" or "Max, are you awake?" and might hear in return, "We're awake, Betsy."

One day in 1985 her parents brought her to the Rosenbach to see Sendak, who was there to read to children. He sat in a large chair in front of a fireplace, and Betsy — when it was her turn — stood beside the chair, and he read *Very Far Away* to her in his gravelly voice. A little boy named Martin, ignored by his mother, runs away to where someone will answer his questions. With a horse, a sparrow, and a cat, Martin finds "very far away" — "many times around the block and two cellar windows from the corner" — where he imagines they will all be happy forever. But soon enough they get on each other's nerves and begin to quarrel and the sparrow decides that very far away isn't far enough, and Martin returns home.

Betsy didn't cry, and so she didn't know — still doesn't — how Sendak knew. Maybe children's book authors have a sixth sense for the hidden emotions of children. He looked at her from behind his large glasses and said, "Child" — she remembers that word so clearly — "Child, it's okay to be sad. You won't always be." He signed the book to her: *For Betsy, especially for Betsy.* Maybe he signed all his books *especially* to anyone, but she believed then — and still does as she opens boxes looking for this book, it's suddenly important that she find it, it's something to *do* — that Maurice Sendak's *especially* was especially for her. What he said to her she didn't tell her friends or her parents or anyone ever. Except Nick, in her mind. Nick, who she pretended — believed — saw everything she did and knew her innermost thoughts.

She finds three boxes of children's books from when she was a girl. More Sendak; and a Dr. Seuss called *The Shape of Me and Other Stuff* ("The shape of water when it drips," she reads now as rain pounds the roof and a drop of water and then another drips from the ceiling); and the book her mother read to her the most, *Winnie-the-Pooh,* "In Which Piglet Is Entirely Surrounded by Water" ("It rained and it rained and it rained"); and a book of poems by Ruth Krauss called *The Cantilever Rainbow* ("was it a part of your childhood yes your story").

She reads and rereads this line — "your childhood yes your story" — and repeats it to herself as she goes downstairs to get a bucket and as she brings it up to catch rainwater. Something to do. She arranges the children's books on built-in shelves by the window, feeling sad, more sad than afraid now, but peacefully so ("Child, it's okay"). She can feel different parts of her negotiating her emotions. Maybe it's hormones, she thinks.

In the fall, back in New York, when Betsy was having a hard time getting through the day — a panic would find her by late afternoon and overtake her by dark — Cal encouraged her to talk to someone. Betsy saw a therapist once a week for two months, a total of eight hours, the equivalent of one workday. He explained to her his belief that every person has an "internal family," inner children, sort of, who need to be in healthy relationships with each other and with the "adult self," the most solid, poised, unafraid, and empathetic part of the person. What he said, and maybe the way he said it, made sense to Betsy. And so her work in therapy, in that small, dimly lit room with a couch, where she sat, and a chair, where her therapist sat — it's so vivid in her mind that she could draw it, if she could draw well — involved a kind of time travel in which her adult self observed and then interceded during pivotal moments from her past when her parts were wounded or afraid — not to change anything, which was impossible, but to comfort, to let Betsy *then* know that everything would be okay.

But — and this was where Betsy stumbled in therapy and why she didn't show up for her ninth session and told Cal she wanted to move back to Philadelphia, which was *not* very far away, was closer, in fact, to her past — would that be the truth? Would everything be okay? What could she say to ten-year-old Betsy, who had recently lost her brother? "Even though Nick just died, and even though your mother will die when you're still a teenager, and even though your father will betray your mother — and you — and even though your relationship with him will never be the same, and even though in your midthirties you will be anxious and indecisive and pregnant before you're married and won't know how to tell the man you love just how afraid you are to have a family, how you're afraid of messing up, because that's what people do, they mess up, and even though on a rainy day in March you won't know what to *do,* you'll feel purposeless and lost — don't worry, child, everything will be okay." Her adult self, when faced with the child she used to be, couldn't quite say this.

Do something, she thinks now.

Start small. Arrange the books. Open one and read to yourself. Then another. Wait for the bucket to fill. Empty it into the sink. Set it back under the drip. Lie on the floor. Close your eyes. Don't do anything. Rest.

College students, Avery thinks even though

she is one, are ridiculous. Neither she nor Peter owns an umbrella, and they are waiting after class to make a run for it across the quad and back to their dorms. It's forty degrees, windy, and pouring, and yet because the calendar says March, because spring break is only a week away, here are intelligent young men and women wearing shorts and *very* short skirts and flip-flops. At least Peter is wearing rain boots and she's wearing a raincoat.

"We should probably go for it," Peter says.

"Two more minutes."

"It could get worse."

"That doesn't seem possible."

"It just got worse."

"That was a wind gust," Avery says.

"Seriously, let's run."

"Wait," Avery says. "Can I use your car?"

"Right now?"

"I feel weird asking."

"Don't feel weird."

"Just for like an hour."

"It's my mother's car."

"Does that mean no?"

"No," Peter says. "I mean, yes, it's cool with me, but do you really want to be driving in this?"

"No, but it's better than biking."

"Where do you need to go?"

"Long story short, there's this man —"

"I *knew* it — another man."

"Peter, are you serious?"

"It's Jerry Ford, isn't it?"

"He's dead."

"Even worse."

"Let me start over," Avery said. "I volunteer at a nursing care facility."

"You do?" Peter says.

"I've been visiting a man who's sick," Avery says. "Every Monday and Wednesday. But I didn't go last week, and I really feel like I should go today, but I usually bike there, and so —"

"No, definitely," Peter says. He gives her his car keys. "It's in the lot behind my dorm."

"Are you sure it isn't weird that I asked?"

"I didn't want to say anything," Peter says, "but I already made you a key for the car, and for my room, and we're having dinner with my parents tonight. I hope yours can make it."

"Shut up," Avery says. "Sometimes I wish you had a pencil neck so I could call you a pencil-necked geek."

"*Geek* will do just fine."

"Thanks for your note, by the way."

"And?"

"Oh, and for your *giant* pencil."

200

Peter laughs. "Screw you."

"Okay, thank you for your *standard* pencil."

"For the record, giant pencils are unwieldy and impractical and not at all beautiful."

"Agreed."

"We'll have to come up with a better word than *standard.*"

"Super-standard."

"I have a Swiss pencil called an Edelweiss."

"Too *Sound of Music.*"

"How about Goldfaber?" Peter says. "It's German."

"Better," Avery says.

"Wait, I have an amazing pencil from Portugal called Fine & Candy."

"And we have a winner," Avery says. "Jesus, we sound like two dudes naming our things."

"I'd rather not think of you with a *thing,*" Peter says. "Though even if you did have one, I'd probably still be into you."

Avery bats her eyelashes and in an exaggeratedly sweet voice says, "That might be the sweetest thing anyone's ever said to me."

"This is *not* getting better," Peter says. "Run on three."

"One more minute."

"One . . . two —"

"Okay, okay, let me put up my hood."

"Three," Peter says, and they run laughing into the rain.

Avery isn't sure who looks worse, her or David. Wind kept blowing her raincoat's hood off her head, and in the twenty-second dash between Peter's mother's Subaru and the nursing care facility's entrance, she got soaked, her long dark hair flat against her head, her jeans heavy and sticking to her legs. But she's never seen David look like he does. He's still in his pajamas, his hair is unkempt, and he needs a shave. Normally, by the time Avery visits him in the afternoon, he's wearing a button-down shirt and pressed pants and his hair is perfectly side-parted, a bit longer on top so that a thin strand falls over his right eye — a Ted Hughes look. Today, however, he's disheveled, as if someone put her hands on David's shoulders and shook him.

He *is* shaking — his hands, his head — and Avery wonders if he didn't take his medication this morning, or maybe he's just getting worse. Of course he's getting worse, she thinks; there will be no getting better.

From his wheelchair, parked purposelessly in the center of the room, he looks up at Avery dripping in the doorway and doesn't seem to recognize her.

"Do you not feel well today?"

"They told me this would happen," he whispers, "but I didn't believe them."

"Who told you what would happen?"

"Someone told me *this* would."

"What would?"

"This!" he yells.

"You can speak," Avery says.

"I can whisper or yell," David whispers. "There's no in-between."

Avery leaves wet boot prints as she walks closer to David's chair. "We need to get you ready," she says. "Dressed, shaved, all that."

"For what?"

"The campaign, of course."

"Didn't I concede?"

"The campaign goes on," Avery says, and with these words David perks up, straightens in his chair.

She thinks about it, she stands in front of his chair, doesn't move, thinks and thinks about it, considers it, but she can't: this is her father, and she just can't undress and dress him.

But she *can* lay out clean clothes on his bed — blue-and-white-striped boxers, navy-blue socks, khakis, white oxford, blue tie. And she *can* shave him: she knows how to shave her own legs, she can shave a man's face. She fills a bowl with warm water and places it in his lap. "Don't spill that," she says, and he says, "My hands have a mind of their own."

She lathers his face and then shaves him with increasing levels of difficulty: the sides of his face, then his neck, then his chin, shaking the razor in the warm water to clean it after every few strokes, and finally between his lips and nose, careful not to nick him.

With a hand towel she wipes away the shaving cream still left on David's neck and by his mouth and ears.

She can brush his teeth, no problem — the campaign goes on. The inside of her father's mouth — so what. If not her, she thinks, then who.

After, she wets a comb and tries to tame a cowlick determined to remain upright; she's tempted to cut it, but in the end she admits defeat and lets it be.

She asks one of the staff members — a pretty woman whose name tag says *Tiffany* — to dress David.

"I tried this morning," Tiffany says, "but he didn't want to."

"He's ready now," Avery says.

Four hallways branch out from a central lobby where nurses and other staff greet visitors and answer phones and where residents congregate, many in wheelchairs, to socialize or sleep. There are more women than men. Some sit by the large glass entrance doors and watch the storm. Rain, especially such heavy rain, on a day that looks more like night, must be incredibly interesting, maybe even moving, Avery thinks, to people who have less rain than most left to see. For a moment Avery sees the rain as if through their eyes, and it *is* moving, and strange, and magical, that water falls from the sky and makes things live and grow. She pushes David along one of the hallways and thinks that wheelchairs too, though man-made, are strange and moving. And aging, what an odd thing that happens to us, utterly strange, shrinking and graying and slowing down. Even her father's disease strikes her as somehow miraculous, that it exists at all, his shaking, his forgetting. She must be in a weird mood, she thinks, her senses and emotions heightened as she pushes David in his chair to the farthest room at the end of a long hallway.

"David Christie," he whispers to a woman sitting in an upright recliner, a small bowl of uneaten rice pudding on her pink plastic lap tray.

The woman smiles but says nothing. Avery

pushes David's chair closer to her. He takes her hand and says, "I hope I can count on you."

"Oh yes, of course," the woman says.

"Your name?" David whispers.

"My friends call me Shirley."

"Shirley," David says. His hand, still holding hers, is shaking.

On to the next room, and the next. He still has it, Avery thinks. And very few people have *it* — a natural charm that draws people in. Kennedy had *it,* so did Jackie, and Bruce Springsteen does, and Julia Roberts, and George Clooney — not her type, but he definitely has *it.* Her mother too. There's something magnetic about her. Men like her, always have. Messy emotions and all. Maybe that's part of the draw, who knows. So she's the daughter of two people who have *it,* but *it* isn't genetic.

David keeps shaking hands, asking the same question: "Can I count on you?"

Whatever they think he means, they say yes, you can count on me.

Some rooms are too dark, and lost in time. TVs blare reruns of *Murder, She Wrote* and *The Dick Van Dyke Show* and *Ironside.* In one room Andy Griffith is a young sheriff in black-and-white Mayberry, and in the next room he has aged a quarter century into

Matlock. Game show contestants scream and jump in place and cry. A woman on a soap opera says to another woman, "Over my cold, dead body will you take my daughter away from me!"

Avery pushes David's wheelchair into a room with a man, older than David, still in bed. David whispers to her, "Not here."

"Are you sure?"

"He's out to get me," David says. Then he says to the man, "Hey, Bill — hey."

"He can't hear you."

"Tell him I'm still standing."

"I hate to break the news," Avery says, "but you're not standing."

David looks down at his chair and smiles. Then he turns back to the man and whispers, "You can't ignore me, Bill."

The man cups his hand around his ear and says, "Huh?"

"Move me closer," David says. Avery pushes his chair into the room and beside the man's bed.

"I'm still here, Bill," David whispers. "I will never concede."

"Who's Bill?" the man says to Avery.

"Don't play dumb," David says to the man.

The man presses his call button, and Avery says, "Let's keep moving."

As she's pushing David's chair toward the lobby, he says, "Be careful — they're watching."

"Who?"

"There are cameras everywhere."

"Don't worry," Avery says. "I took care of that."

"Thank you," David says. "I knew I could trust you."

They pause in the lobby and listen to rain blow against windows and glass doors. A flash of lightning, and the lights flicker. "It's coming," David says.

"We're gonna need a bigger boat," Avery says. When David doesn't react, she says, "That's from *Jaws.*"

"First date we went on after we had kids."

"That's great that you remember."

"My son was seven and my daughter was one, I think."

"Do you know who I am?"

"My chief of staff," he says. "My chief of everything."

"My name," she says.

"Avery who goes to college."

David points to a nurse behind the large desk near the entrance. She's tall and thin, her gray hair pulled back into a bun. "Go tell her," David says.

"Tell her what?"

"What's going on."

"Can you be more specific?"

"Bill," he says.

"I don't think Bill's going to give us any trouble."

"She'll know what to do."

"What should I say?"

"You'll know."

Avery walks toward the nurse with no idea what to say. She can't possibly say that a man not named Bill is out to get David, and she can't say that David *believes* that a man not named Bill is out to get him, and she can't stand in front of the nurse and pretend to speak to her — move her mouth, gesture with her hands — for David's benefit, or else the nurse will throw her out. Maybe: "Mr. Christie is a little off today." Maybe: "I'm worried about Mr. Christie." Maybe: "I'm worried about my father."

She says, "May I please have a cup of water — for Mr. Christie. I'm visiting with him today, and he said he's thirsty."

"Sure," the nurse says, and brings Avery a paper cup filled with cold water. "Anything else, let us know."

"Thank you," Avery says.

But when Avery tries to give David the water, holding the cup near his lips, he turns his head and pinches his mouth shut like a child who doesn't want to take his medicine. "They got to her," he says. "She's one of them now."

"She seems very nice," Avery says.

David's eyes narrow. "They didn't get to *you,* did they?"

"Absolutely not."

"Take me back to my room."

When they're in his room, David asks Avery to close the door. "I need you to help me," he says.

"Anything," Avery says.

"My raincoat."

"Are you cold?"

"Please, my raincoat."

Avery finds a long beige raincoat in the closet. "Burberry — very nice," she says. She leans David forward in his chair, fits the coat behind him, helps his arms through the sleeves, tries to straighten it out as much as possible.

"Better?" she says.

"Better," he whispers. "But now I need to get out."

"It's not the best weather for a walk, you know."

"Listen to me," he whispers. "I need you to get me *out* of here."

■ ■ ■ ■

I'm taking Mr. Christie out for a few hours.

Mr. Christie asked me to take him out —
only for a few hours.

I'm taking Mr. Christie for a drive.

This storm, I know, but I'll have him back
in a few hours.

I'm taking my father out. We'll be back
later.

Yes, my father.

You've seen me here.

We don't have the same name.

Because I changed it.

Because I wanted to.

Not that daughter. His other daughter.

For the past month Avery has worried
about running into *that* daughter, but she
must visit on weekends.

She pushes David's wheelchair past the
nurses' station, practicing in her mind what
she might say. She parks him beside the
residents watching the rain. Best to do this
in stages, she thinks. She *is* wearing her
raincoat, and so is David, and that might
raise suspicions, but before anyone has a
chance to question her, she thinks: Screw
this, I *am* his daughter, and pushes his chair
outside.

Stages, she thinks. Take it slow.

They pause outside the entrance, under a carport, watching the storm. She keeps glancing back at the front desk, waiting for the tall nurse with gray hair to turn away or walk away or —

The nurse answers the phone and then starts looking through some files. *Now,* Avery thinks.

She speed-walks to the Subaru, rain pelting her face, and then fumbles with the keys. She opens the front passenger door, moves David's wheelchair closer to the car, locks the wheels, straddles the chair's footrest, puts her arms around her father, bends her knees, and pulls her father to his feet. She turns him and lowers him into the car, then lifts his legs in. She makes sure he's seated straight and fastens his seat belt. She pulls up on the wheelchair's seat — she has watched the nurses do this — and it folds in on itself, its sides pressed together; she lifts it into the back of the Outback. She hurries around to the driver side and gets into the car, soaked but exhilarated at having gotten this far.

She imagines someone knocking on the car window, and what she would say: "He's my father. I'm his daughter." Remember those two words, *father* and *daughter,* and everything will be okay. Those two words are the truth, and you can't get in trouble for stating the truth.

Actually, she thinks, you can.

"So," she says to her father, "where would you like to go?"

"Anywhere," he whispers. "Away from here."

Avery is giving David a tour of campus. Not that they can see much with the rain falling so hard. Even on high, the wipers can't keep the windshield clear. Driving's making Avery dizzy. She points out her dorm, the bookstore, and the bust of James Buchanan, which drunk students have been peeing on for over one hundred years. "That's the library," she says. "There's this nook no one seems to know about except me. It's dark, and if you stay still the motion-sensor lights don't come on. You have to use the light from your phone to read. This is probably really boring, huh."

"I'm sorry," David whispers. "Sometimes I get lost."

"Me too."

"I know this place," David says.

"Maybe you've been here before," Avery says, and immediately regrets it. She's fishing; she knows that. What does she expect

— or want — him to say? *Yes, it's all coming back to me now. My wife used to teach here. She died years ago. So did my son. But I have two daughters still alive, and I know you're one of them. I'm sorry I wasn't a father to you. It's no excuse, but I was in pain, I was angry, I was humiliated, I was guilty, and I needed to take it out on someone, and it shouldn't have been you. But here we are now, so let's make up for lost time.*

"I had a dream about this place," he says. "Are you part of the dream?"

"I'm real," Avery says.

"Tell me the truth." David's head shakes in a no motion. His hands are crossed on his lap as if each is trying to hold the other still.

"The truth?" Avery says.

"Should we concede?"

"As your chief of everything, my advice is: you'll know when it's time."

"I don't feel like stumping today."

"Let's get lunch."

"Not at the state fair."

"The state fair's rained out," Avery says. "I know this great taco place. Do you like tacos?"

"I don't remember," David says.

The taco place, called Angel Tacos, probably should have been called Angel's Tacos because the owner's name is Angel, but it sounds better without the possessive, Avery thinks, because it makes the tacos sound as if they're heavenly good. And they are. Peter was the one who took Avery to Angel Tacos — one point for him for being a first-year and already knowing about a taco place not many students know about.

She drives away from campus and through Buchanan, past row homes, people smoking on porches, watching the storm.

She thought she knew where the taco place was, but now that she's in the vicinity — she thinks she is, anyway — she's not so sure. She drives carefully down a long, steep hill, and at the bottom, after driving slowly through a deep puddle, she pulls the car over to wait out the rain — not that it seems to be letting up — and to try to remember whether to turn right or left at the bodega where students buy cigarettes and rolling papers.

She turns off the wipers. "Looks like we're in a car wash," she says, and then she and her father are quiet, just the rain against the car, and maybe they can stay here for a while, forget lunch, maybe she should turn to him and say those two words, *father, daughter* — four words, *my father, your daughter* — eight words, *you are my father, I am your daughter.* But she doesn't want to confuse him, or frighten him, and even if he does understand, he might forget a few minutes later.

"Tell me the truth," he whispers.

"Do you remember your name?"

"David."

"Last name?"

"David . . ." He stares at the rain through the windshield. Avery looks where he's looking, but it makes her dizzy. She looks back at him. "David . . ."

"Christie," she says.

"Am I married?"

"You were."

"I'm sorry if I've asked you these questions before."

"It's okay."

"Remind me of your name."

"Avery."

"Avery who goes to college."

"My last name is Modern," Avery says.

"Avery Modern," David whispers.

"Actually," Avery says, but pauses, unsure what comes next, if anything should. She imagines saying, "Actually, my last name used to be Bautista-Christie."

Pounding on her window startles Avery. She can make out a blurry man. She thinks:

Carjack.

The man bangs on the window again.

Maybe he's in trouble, she thinks. She rolls down the window a few inches and rain blows into her face. He's a middle-aged white man with a ponytail and a long beard. He looks like Willie Nelson, but taller.

"Get out of the car!"

"I don't know you," she says. Before she can locate the power-lock button, the man pulls open her door.

He's standing in water above his knees.

"Flash flood," he says. "You need to get out of this vehicle."

The man lifts Avery from the car and carries her through the water to a Ford pickup a few feet away. Two children, a boy and a girl in school uniforms, probably the man's kids, sit in the passenger seat. The man lays Avery in the truck bed and says, "Don't move."

Avery pulls up her hood and watches the man wade back to the Subaru to get David. "He can't walk," she calls out to the man, but he doesn't seem to hear her.

Shit, she thinks. Shit. Fuck.

Peter. His mother's car.

Her father.

She tries to think of a plan. What to tell Peter. How to get her father back. What to say to the nursing staff.

When the man lays David next to her, Avery says, "His wheelchair is in the back. I can't leave it."

"He can get it later."

"I can't leave it."

The man goes back to get the wheelchair. "Thank you," Avery calls out, but her words seem to get lost in the wind and rain. David's hair is soaked flat, but somehow — maybe it's the Burberry — he manages to look not *too* bad. She puts her arm around him. The children turn to look at Avery and David, then turn away again.

"This is real," he whispers.

"Yes," she says.

"Are you okay?"

"Are *you* okay?"

He smiles and says, "I think it's time to concede."

The man carries the folded wheelchair above the water and lays it on the truck bed. He tries to start his truck, but the engine won't turn.

He tries again. Nothing.

On the third try, it starts, and he drives them away from the water deepening around them.

■ ■ ■ ■

PART FIVE:
DAUGHTERS

1993–2008

■ ■ ■ ■

JANUARY 20, 1993

First they'd sat in traffic leaving DC, then they'd sat in traffic on the Brooklyn-Queens Expressway, and now, six hours after Tim Swisher had picked up David, they were finally in Queens. The drive should have taken four hours. They'd left at five thirty, when it was still dark, and now it was approaching noon. It had been Tim's idea to take his car, and for David to wear a baseball hat; that way, David wouldn't be recognized. Not that anyone was thinking about him today. He hadn't shaved in two weeks, and that would help too, just in case.

The capital had been a zoo the past two days, one million people on the National Mall, Michael Jackson, Barbra Streisand, Bob Dylan, Tony Bennett, Bill Cosby, American entertainment royalty, presidential pomp and circumstance. David couldn't wait to get out of DC, but now that he was

221

in Queens, he didn't want to be there either. He didn't want to be anywhere except home in Philadelphia, where he wasn't welcome.

Tim, driving slowly through Jackson Heights, the elevated train passing above them, looked at the address he'd written on the piece of paper on his lap. Tim Swisher, no longer David's body man, but still willing to do this. Maybe he felt responsible; he had to have known. David had told him that none of this was *his* fault. He had been David's keeper, politically speaking, but not his keeper otherwise. Now that he didn't work for David, he offered his opinions about personal matters, sometimes unsolicited. Which was why they were here.

She had gotten in touch with Tim — David wouldn't have any contact with her — to say that David's daughter, *their* daughter, was five months old, and no matter what else was happening in his life, he should see her. Tim took a chance and brought it up with David.

"I won't see that woman."

"I know, but David —"

"I'm trying to move forward."

"She's just a baby."

"She's not *just* a baby."

"With all due respect," Tim said, "the baby didn't do anything wrong."

"I'll make sure she's taken care of."

"David, you should see her."

"Danielle's not doing well," David said.

"I understand," Tim said. "I won't bring it up again."

But as the inauguration approached, David couldn't stand the thought of being in DC, so he called Tim and asked him to arrange things. He would see the baby, and Danielle wouldn't have to know — they were separated, after all. The only condition, he told Tim, was that he wouldn't have to see *her.*

Tim knew who David meant, and exactly how to arrange things, and here they were.

"This is the address," Tim said.

But before Tim parked the car, David said, "Not here. Park at the end of the street."

"She said she'd leave."

"I won't have any interaction with her," David said. "None."

Tim circled around the block and parked at the other end of the street, outside a bodega. "I'll be back in a few," he said.

David could hear a train arriving at the Roosevelt Avenue station around the corner. He pulled down the passenger side's sun visor and looked into its mirror. There was more gray in his beard than on his head. If

223

only he could turn gray overnight, turn old, turn sick, take it from Danielle, he would. He lowered his hat so that it cast a shadow over his face. He should have brought sunglasses.

He was far enough away that she wouldn't be able to see him, but he could see her come out of the building — a brick row home that looked almost identical to those around it. She sat on the stoop. Then he saw Tim walk down the steps, past her, and back to the car.

David rolled down the window. "Make her leave."

"She's pretty emotional right now."

"I don't care. Make her go somewhere."

"She said it's her apartment, she lives there. I reminded her what we agreed to, and she said she'd wait on the stoop."

"I'll leave right now," David said. "Turn around and head back to DC."

"How long should I tell her to be gone?"

"Twenty minutes."

David watched Tim speak to her. She stood as if to leave, but sat down again; she covered her face with her hands.

Tim sat beside her and put his hand on her shoulder. He was good at reasoning with people; he had a calming voice. He'd make a good politician, David thought, if only he weren't so honest.

After a few minutes, she stood and walked away.

Tim signaled to David, who got out of the car and walked to the building. From the stoop he could see her standing on the corner without a coat and — she had to be kidding — barefoot. She was pacing and walking in circles — to keep warm or, David guessed, to give the impression of being cold. It was January, but forty degrees. She wouldn't get frostbite.

The stairs up to the third floor were creaky; the hallways were dark. The apartment door, ajar, opened onto a small living room, behind that a kitchenette. Wood alphabet blocks, plastic rattles and rings, and stuffed animals were in neat piles on the rug and inside a playpen. The TV was on, its volume low. Reverend Billy Graham was praying for President Bush, who would be president for ten more minutes, and for President-Elect Clinton, who sat beside his wife and daughter. David was surprised to find the apartment so tidy, even though she — he would not think her name — had been one of the cleanest women he'd ever known. Her body never smelled; she never had morning breath; he'd never seen a hair under her arms or felt stubble on her legs;

her fingernail and toenail polish was never chipped. Emotionally, she could be messy; physically, not.

A woman was in the apartment, holding the baby. She was older than David but not old enough to be the child's grandmother, so David assumed she was a nanny or a sitter. She said hello but not her name. David didn't ask who she was; his attention was focused on the baby. The truth was, he could now admit, he did want to see her. Not out of love — he didn't know how to love this child — but out of disbelief. He knew he was the father, there was no question of that now, he'd taken a paternity test, but he wanted to see for himself, and yes, those were his eyes, and now the nanny — if that was who she was — handed him the baby and he felt the weight of a baby for the first time since the campaign, but no, it didn't bring him back to that, fuck the campaign, it reminded him of holding Nick, and then Betsy, and God if he could go back in time, never speak to that woman, never call her, throw away the note. Except that would mean this baby would not exist; it would be like killing her. A terrible thought, but he couldn't help it. If only, God forgive him, he could exchange this child for Nick, this one he never wanted for the one he lost.

It was impossible to look into this child's eyes, which were his, and not associate them with his son's death. He would never be able to separate Nick from this, and this from Danielle; it was all one cancer that had started to grow in 1984.

Tim was waiting in the bedroom, and the nanny was in the kitchenette. David moved his face close to the baby and smelled her breath, and the baby smiled. He held her up high and looked at her from that angle — she was wearing white pajamas — but he could see in his peripheral vision Clinton taking off his overcoat, and now he was standing between his wife and daughter. David got up and turned off the TV.

But as soon as the screen went dark, he changed his mind; he wanted to see. He turned the TV back on. Clinton laid his left hand on a Bible his wife held open for him; he raised his right hand. He repeated what Chief Justice Rehnquist said, and just like that, with the words *So help me God,* William Jefferson Clinton was president of the United States and George Herbert Walker Bush was not.

David turned the TV off again.

The baby was starting to fuss in his arms. She touched his beard, looked confused, touched it again, then started to cry. He was out of practice making a baby stop crying. He sat on the couch and held the baby on his lap and said her name, Avery, that was fine, it was all right to say it, but she kept crying.

The nanny brought David a bottle, and he held it to Avery's mouth.

"There you go," the nanny said. "All better now. You wanted your mommy's milk, didn't you?"

David dropped the bottle, as if it were poison, and this startled the baby; she started to cry again.

"I'm sorry," he said.

The nanny picked up the bottle and brought it to the sink to wash the nipple.

When she brought the bottle back to David, he said, "I have to go."

He passed her the baby, and he knew then that he would never see this child again.

When David left, she was sitting on the stoop, shivering. He and Tim Swisher walked past her and down the street to the car, and then they started the long drive back to Washington.

MARCH 14, 1993

Everyone was buried; at least Danielle wasn't the only one.

Even God had declared a snow day. Danielle heard it on the radio: Catholics in the Archdiocese of Philadelphia had been granted dispensation from attending Mass.

And Danielle had granted Betsy dispensation from her duties as caretaker for her mother — no longer chemo-sick, just cancer-sick. She had encouraged Betsy to get away — had insisted — and finally Betsy relented and went to visit a friend in San Francisco. She, for one, was not being buried; she had escaped all this, but who knew when she would be able to fly home.

Danielle looked out her bedroom window: everything was white. A blizzard one week before spring. It had snowed all day yesterday and hadn't stopped yet, and today the snow was so deep that most neighbors, she could see, had given up on shoveling. She had slept late, and now lunchtime had passed — she had eaten only half of a banana — and the blizzard made it feel okay to get back into bed. She wasn't in *too* much pain — the morphine lollipop helped — but the medicine made her dizzy and it was increasingly difficult to walk or stand or read. Still, she tried to read; she wouldn't give that up.

Mostly what she felt was tired. She'd been sleeping off and on day and night, a few hours awake, a few hours asleep. Her favorite hour, she'd discovered, was 4:00 AM, before most others were awake — waiting for and then seeing the first glow of a new day's light. Her least favorite was one hour earlier, 3:00 AM, that no-man's-land between night and morning, which was just plain lonely. So lonely that with Betsy away, Danielle had been tempted to call David, had wished that he might call her. He had called regularly the first weeks after their separation to see how she was feeling, but she tended not to answer, instead listening to his voice as he left a message. Their answering machine's greeting used to be David's voice, but a week after he moved out, Danielle recorded a new one. She kept it simple: "We're not here, please leave a message." Callers could figure out for themselves whom *we* now included and did not. Some nights, during her least favorite hour, she would play back David's messages on low volume so that Betsy wouldn't hear.

She loved the old David enough to hate the new David all the more. "What did you do to my husband?" she wanted to scream at him, as if they were two separate people, when really they were both inside him — the two Davids. There were more than two, of course: the David she had married, David the father, David the lawyer, David who had lost his son, David the senator, David the presidential candidate, and the David she didn't know, David between August and December 1991 — four months during which, she tried to believe, an imposter had taken over her husband's body.

Now: Sad David. David the penitent. David who didn't live here anymore.

And who was *she* now? She was separated from her husband. She was sometimes humiliated — even though she had done nothing wrong. She was no longer a professor. In another six to eight months, best guess, she would no longer be a cancer patient. In another six to eight months, best guess, she would no longer be a mother. Would no longer be anything. But today, right now, she was a fifty-four-year-old woman in her pajamas and robe, getting back into bed at 2:00 PM after having sucked on a morphine lollipop.

She could no longer get through full plays — dizziness, blurred vision — and so she had stacked a dozen or so of her favorites on her bedside table and read passages from each, and it seemed to her now, as she dipped into Sophocles and Shakespeare and O'Neill and Miller and Williams and Mamet, that they were all one long, strange play, and that her life itself — maybe it was the morphine that made her feel his way — was a play, and that she was in its final act, and the rooms of this house were its set. Act whatever, in which our protagonist can't get through more than a few sentences at a time, in which our protagonist opens book after book and for only the second time in her life — the first was after her son died — doesn't care much for reading about made-up people in made-up dramas, an activity that once brought so much meaning to her life. A blizzard was burying her, and beautiful words couldn't change much.

I should have written a play, she thought. The play I will never have time now to write. If this were the final act of the play, she thought, it wouldn't be very interesting

— a sick woman in bed as another afternoon slips away. The protagonist must *do* something.

She got out of bed, unsteady on her feet, and went looking for props. A good scene needed props. She walked down the hallway to David's office, opened the door, but did not go in. His desk, still there. His chair. A cup of pens on the desk. A legal pad. A phone. Some of his books remained, but most shelves were empty. Some of his clothes still hung in his bedroom closet, but no suits and absolutely no ties — nothing that might remind her. He'd left behind some polo shirts and sweaters and sweatshirts, and she hadn't said: "Take them too. Take everything." He'd left behind a toothbrush, a razor, shaving cream, deodorant (from time to time, she smelled it), but she had put his toiletries into a box. That he'd left behind anything, that she'd let him, was maybe a sign of hope that they could fix this. She did hope — at first. Until the final blow — the baby. Some things you could not fix, could not make go away.

She stepped into David's office, what had been his, and stood there a moment. On the other side of the window behind David's desk the world was white and more white. She walked to the desk and sat. She took a pen from the pen cup. On the legal pad she wrote the date. Then what? *Dear David? Dear Betsy? Dear Living?* She tried to focus her vision. No, she would never write a note or a play or a memoir — her version of the story. Books would be written about David, she was sure. Even *she,* the one whose name she tried not to think, might write a book. It wasn't fair, Danielle thought, that *she* would get to live, her life would go on, while Danielle —

She picked up the phone and dialed information. When asked what city, she said, "Jackson Heights, New York." When asked what listing, she brought herself to say the name.

"Please hold for the number."

A computerized voice recited the number, but Danielle did not write it down, she did not want to see it, wanted no record of it. Instead, she pressed the button on the phone to be connected, and then suddenly the phone was ringing — somewhere in Queens — and Danielle still wasn't sure what she would say. It felt better to be angry with *her,* to make *her* the only villain. That way, she and David could be on the same team again.

Hello, this is Danielle Christie. I need to say a few things to you.

She could hang up on Danielle. Then what?

This is Danielle Christie. I may not be alive much longer, but I want to make sure you hear this from me.

Of course she would hang up.

Danielle had waited five rings now, and she expected to hear *her* voice on an answering machine. Yes, then she could say everything she wanted.

What you did was immoral, and what you did after — talking to tabloids instead of just going away and leaving us alone — was just as terrible. You are a sick person. You will never know the pain you have caused my family. You will never know.

But the phone kept ringing, it was up to a dozen now, still no answering machine — and then a loud *crack,* what sounded like a cannon fired. It frightened Danielle so much that she dropped the receiver.

She went to the window, but nothing seemed to be different: children built snowmen and threw snowballs at each other and at lampposts and trees.

Then she heard a low but growing rumble and realized what it was.

Thunder during a blizzard. She knew that was possible but had never heard it before. She picked up the receiver but heard nothing. She put it in its cradle, then picked it up again. Still nothing. She tried a lamp, then another; the power had gone out.

She was tired and wanted to get back into bed, but the sun was out — during a blizzard — and she needed to see this, not just through a window. She gathered enough energy to put on boots — she didn't bother to tie the laces — and a winter coat, and she walked slowly down the stairs and out onto the stoop. Watching the children play, she remembered Nick and Betsy playing on this same street ten years earlier, during another huge snowstorm. The cars were buried in snow, and there was nothing that seemed to set the two days apart in time — except Danielle's age.

She looked up at the snow falling. A strange miracle, snow. Even explainable things could be miraculous.

She couldn't read much anymore, she wasn't even that interested in reading, she was too tired, and that was how she knew, how she really knew, that what the doctors had told her was true: she was not long for this world.

That phrase — *not long for this world* — was beautiful, she felt, as she looked up into the swirling snow. It meant: I won't be in this world for long. But she heard something closer to: I long for this world. But what she longed for was a world already gone — when Nick was here, and her children were children, and David was the David she knew and trusted. If she didn't look down at how bony her hands had become, and if she didn't reach up to touch her face, too thin, or her hair, too brittle, and if she didn't touch her lips, too dry, she might be able to believe today was years ago. That, she decided, would be a kind of heaven — to be able to go back in time and relive just one day, before anything went wrong, before they even imagined that it could.

She went inside and took off her boots and her coat. She went up to bed, where within minutes she fell asleep.

When she woke, it was dark — outside and inside. She was thirsty, and the pain was working its way back through her body. She walked through the dark to the bathroom for a glass of water. She found candles, brought them downstairs, and lit them. After starting a fire in the fireplace, she tried to get comfortable on the couch under two blankets.

And then, just as she was about to fall asleep again, the lights came back on and the phone was ringing.

She wrapped one of the blankets around her and went to the phone in the kitchen. She let it ring until she heard her own voice on the answering machine. "We're not here . . ."

Following the beep, there was a pause. Then she heard David's voice. "It's me," he said. "I just wanted to check on you."

Danielle picked up the phone. "David," she said.

"What's wrong?" he said.

"Nothing."

"You sound like you're crying."

After a moment he said, "I've been trying to reach you."

She couldn't get out any words. David said, "Honey, are you still there?"

"I'm still here," she said.

OCTOBER 23, 1996

Betsy's roommate, her fourth in just over three years at Columbia, was hovering. Her previous roommates had been distant, as if afraid of her, but this one was the opposite: she liked to poke, prod, intrude; she asked too many questions; she was the nosiest person Betsy had ever met. Her name was Virginia, and some people called her Gin, but she was from Montana, and some people called her Montana. Betsy thought of her simply as the roommate. It was hard not to think about her; she was always there.

Now, for example: hovering over Betsy as she packed a bag. The roommate was dressed as a Bond girl — specifically, Honey Ryder, played by Ursula Andress in 1962's *Dr. No.* She planned to wear the costume every day for the next week. The temperature was around fifty, but still, the roommate was wearing a white bikini and a white belt above her bikini bottom and a brown leather holster for a plastic knife, all of which Andress had worn during a "famous" beach scene, the roommate had explained to Betsy. She had worn this outfit to her classes.

"When people ask who I'm supposed to be," she said now, "I never say Honey Ryder, which is like a porn star's name. I say Ursula Andress, which I guess could be a porn star's name too — you know, because *Andress* sounds like *undress*. But I just love her. I wish my last name were Andress." The roommate had declared this, almost word for word, that morning when Betsy first saw her costume, and Betsy now said the same thing she'd said that morning: "You're old enough to change your name, you know."

"Would you ever change your name?"

This, Betsy knew, after two months as the roommate's roommate, was a teaser question intended to elicit personal information.

"I like my name," Betsy said.

"Are you an Elizabeth?"

"You've asked me that before," Betsy said.

"Oh, sorry."

"I'm just Betsy."

"Because usually when you meet a Betsy, she's an Elizabeth."

Betsy wanted to say, "Usually you don't

meet a Virginia from Montana," but she knew this could elicit a long monologue from the roommate about her family history, which would lead to the story of how her parents got divorced but then remarried each other, which would lead to various stories of her own romantic life, how she dated only older men, including one of her professors, stories she'd already told Betsy who knew how many times. Betsy didn't know what to believe anyway. She had come to assume that everyone was lying, that people had ulterior motives, that no one could be trusted.

"Listen, I was thinking, maybe you want some company."

"Thanks, but I may stay only one night."

"I don't really know Philadelphia," the roommate said.

"Maybe next time."

Betsy grabbed a few books from her desk and a sweater from her drawer, put them into her bag, and zipped it closed.

The roommate was standing in front of the door. "Are you sure? I wouldn't mind going."

"Thanks, really, but I'd like to spend some quality time with my dad."

There — she'd said it. Brought *him* up. Which she knew would give the roommate an opening to say:

"What's he like — your father?"

Betsy paused as if trying to find just the right words. "He's lonely and has no friends, except Swish, which is the dog he recently got — because he's lonely. He's handsome, and he's dated a few women since my mother died — I told you she died, right? — and I've met a few by accident, but he wasn't really interested in them, I could tell, because he still loves my mother."

For the first time in two months, the roommate was speechless.

"Any other questions about my father?" Betsy said.

She had lied, of course. Her father did have a few friends, including Tim Swisher — such a good friend he didn't mind a dog being named after him. And the part about quality time with her father — it *was* what she wanted, but she didn't know what that meant anymore. He *was* lonely, and she didn't know how to be around him. Sometimes she believed that he *should* be lonely, not as some kind of punishment but because — she didn't know why, it just seemed right, for now. He was practicing law again. Like Betsy, he spent too much time working. In the three years Betsy had been in college, she and her father had drifted from each other. They hadn't become strangers, but their conversations were brief and remained safely on the surface of things — her classes, his work, the dog. Never politics, especially not now, during the homestretch of an election season. Not that there was much suspense: Dole had no chance, Clinton would be reelected in a landslide, anyone could see that. Sometimes, they talked about Nick. Sometimes, by accident, awkwardly, about her mother.

As the train approached Philadelphia, her stomach went cold — a nervous feeling she hated. She remembered that she had two chocolate chip cookies in her bag. She ate half of one and put the uneaten half back into her bag. She felt a little better. But then she felt worse again, and so she ate the other half of the first cookie, and then she ate the second cookie, and then the train pulled into Thirtieth Street Station in Philadelphia, but she didn't move. She sat there, chewing the last of the second cookie, as passengers walked down the aisle and off the train.

An hour later she got off in Buchanan. She'd done this before, but not in a few years. The first year after her mother died, she would take the train to Buchanan and walk from the station to the college where her mother had taught, and then walk around campus. She could have been a student there, and sometimes pretended that she was. She would go to the library and do her homework there. She would look in the stacks for her mother's book about tragedy. She didn't go into the building where her mother's office had been for fear that someone might recognize her.

It was dusk now, and she should be at home; her father would wonder where she was. She didn't want to walk around Buchanan College; she didn't know what she wanted except not to be home.

She walked through the streets of Buchanan with no plan, no destination. Her father used to do something like this — go for a run without a plan, just run wherever he felt like it, turn here, go straight for a while, turn there, and see where fate, if that was what it was, led him. She did that now — except she walked. It was scary not knowing exactly where she was or where she was going or for how long she'd do this or when she'd be able to get the next train home or how worried her father might be, but then she felt it — the Nick-feeling, as if he were with her or watching her. A good feeling.

And then she saw a bright light and walked toward it.

As she got closer, she saw the sign: *Wheatland.*

Her mother had taught for over twenty years at a college named after James Buchanan, and yet Betsy knew very little about him, except that he had preceded Lincoln.

Betsy could feel the ghosts inside Wheatland: hats and coats still hung on hooks; calling cards in the calling card dish by the front entrance; unfinished letters beside dry quills on the desk Buchanan used in the White House; an unopened bottle of wine dated 1827; two depressions in the padded prayer bench where Buchanan's niece used to kneel; empty chamber pots; an empty cup on Buchanan's shaving desk; empty beds perfectly made; the small tin tub where Buchanan stood to bathe; a large brass tub and above it the showerhead through which warmed rainwater fell; a portrait of two boys, Buchanan's niece's sons, already dead from rheumatic fever by the time the artist created their likeness, the sea and a rocky shoreline in the background. The docent, an old man dressed in nineteenth-century fashion, kept saying "you all" even though Betsy was the only one on the tour — the last of the day. As Betsy walked through the house, she imagined that time had not passed, that all time was happening at once, that every moment lasted forever: James Buchanan was still and would always be washing his gouty feet, and always listening to his niece play the piano, and always hanging his coat on the coatrack by the front door, and always writing his memoir, and always dying in his bed with a view of the lawn and the trees, his lungs and heart failing; he would always be sipping wine and warming his bed and taking his last breath.

When Betsy arrived home, her father was waiting at the door. "I thought you'd be home earlier."

"I missed my train."

He asked what she wanted for dinner, and she said, "Sorry, I made plans," and he said, "Maybe tomorrow night," and she said, "Actually, I may need to head back tomorrow for a study group," and he said, "Breakfast, then."

Betsy had no plans but went out anyway. She went to a bar, ordered a beer, and took her time drinking it. Later, in Rittenhouse Square, she sat on a bench under a lamp and read. She waited until ten o'clock before walking home.

There was egg on the side of the house.

She didn't believe that it had been a random prank. Quietly she went inside and down to the basement, where she filled a bucket with warm soapy water. She found a rag, carried the rag and bucket outside, and wiped the bricks and windows, but this only seemed to make it worse, the egg spreading. She wiped so hard that she made a hole in the rag.

The front door opened. Under the porch light she could see more gray in her father's hair. "Come in," he said.

"Just let me clean this."

"Don't worry about it."

"Stupid kids," she said. "It's not even Halloween yet."

She continued scrubbing until her father took the rag from her. "It's late," he said. "Please come in now."

DECEMBER 17, 1999

It was parents' day, but in her mind — and aloud — Avery kept calling it *parent* day. It was the last day of school before break, a week before Christmas Eve. Avery, who already knew there was no Santa Claus, had asked her mother for the new Harry Potter — her mother had read to her the first two, and in the fall, Avery, a great reader for seven years old, had read the third on her own — and she was disappointed when her mother told her that the fourth book did not exist yet, that it wouldn't be published until next year. She asked instead for *Anne of Green Gables* and *The Secret Garden* and *James and the Giant Peach.* Her mother said, "You know you're not an orphan, right?" and Avery said, "I know," and her mother said, "Then why so many books about orphans?" and Avery said, "I didn't *know* they were all about orphans."

Except she did; she *was* interested in orphans. She found the idea of being an orphan, at least in the cases of Harry Potter and Pippi Longstocking, to be more exciting than frightening. She never wanted her mother to die — *Bambi* and *Dumbo* and *The Lion King* had made her cry — but sometimes she imagined that for *some* reason she was alone, and therefore special, and had secret powers, and was worthy of being written about in books.

She'd written a book for parent day — all second graders did — but it had to be a *non*fiction book, meaning it had to be true, and it had to be about your family, and so she'd written five pages — three complete sentences and a drawing on each page — about how her favorite thing to do was fall asleep knowing her mother was still up, and some mornings she woke first and got into bed with her mother and watched her sleep and sometimes fell back asleep herself, and when Avery woke again her mother was right there watching her. She knew how to draw a really good bed with details like bedposts and even the pink flowers on the bedspread, and she gave her mother long dark hair — she liked her mother's hair — even though her mother pulled her hair back before bed.

The children sat on a large oval rug in the center of the classroom and read their books aloud to their parents. Some kids had a mom and a dad there, some had just a dad there, some had just a mom there, some had two moms, no one had two dads there, though Avery understood — her mother had explained all this to her — that some kids, maybe no one in her class, had two dads, and that was okay, there were many kinds of families.

Like theirs, her mother had told her. Avery had both a mother and a father, but she was being *raised* by her mother. As soon as she was old enough, around when she was three, she had asked where her father was, and her mother had said, "Your father had some difficult things happen, and right now he's sad and needs to try to feel better, but when he's better, I'm sure he'll come to see you."

A few days later Avery asked, "What difficult things?"

Her mother thought about her answer for longer than usual, and Avery waited. Then her mother said, "He made some mistakes, and was very hard on himself." Avery wanted to know what mistakes, and her mother said, "Sometimes people make complicated choices," an answer Avery found too complicated to understand.

When she was five, she finally thought she understood. She asked if her father had died.

No, her mother told her — he was alive.

Now, Avery read her nonfiction book to her mother, while her classmates did the same, and she could see that her mother was pleased. Avery knew that her mother's tears were happy, not sad — her mother had explained the difference.

When Avery finished reading, the boy sitting beside her looked at her book's cover — a drawing of her and her mother beneath the title *My Family* — and said, "You forgot to draw your dad."

Avery looked at her mother. Then she glanced at some of the other covers around her: each had two parents and sometimes brothers and sisters, and her cover seemed plain in comparison. "Why don't we add him," her mother said, and Avery shrugged, which was not a yes, but not a no. Her mother asked the teacher for a box of crayons, and she brought it to Avery and sat on the big circle rug and watched Avery draw. Because she didn't know what her father looked like, Avery gave him red hair like Pippi Longstocking and round glasses like Harry Potter and made him very tall and gave him a tie. But before she had finished, her mother said, "He has brown hair, and he doesn't wear glasses," and now Avery started to get upset, it was impossible to erase crayon, and maybe her mother could see Avery's eyes filling, because she said, "It's okay, it's good the way it is, keep going." Avery didn't want to, and so her mother finished the drawing, coloring the tie blue and trying her best to change the hair from red to brown.

Avery had drawn her father all the way on the right side of the cover — she and her mother were in the middle — and her mother drew a jump rope in her father's hands even though his hands were at his sides, and connected the jump rope to Avery's hands, even though she'd never jumped rope in her life, and the cover looked weird, it was ruined, but she didn't want her mother to see her upset, so she excused herself to the bathroom, and took her time, and when she came out her mother was still working on the cover, as if she were the child. She had drawn a house and a sun and a partly cloudy sky.

That night, her mother brought Avery a shoe box; inside were photos of her father — not real photos but cutouts from newspapers and books. He did have brown hair, just as her mother had drawn it on Avery's cover, and he didn't have glasses, and he was wearing a tie, and he was handsome and looked like a nice man — he was smiling — and her mother said, "This is your father, and he will always be your father. I can tell you more about him as you get older. Would you like that?"

Avery shrugged, which was not yes, not no. One part of her did want to know more, and another part of her — the part that preferred to imagine her father — did not.

OCTOBER 18, 2000

The things you hide; the things you tell no one; the things you take to the grave. Maybe the dead could see. David wondered about that. He imagined that Nick was watching. Especially during his early-morning runs along the river with Swish, watching the sun rise over the water. He didn't pray, but sometimes he talked to Nick — which was, for David, a kind of prayer. Are you there? Are you somewhere? Can you see me? Even when I hide my hands in my pockets, can you see the tremors? So slight someone might not notice. Still, he hid his hands.

When he used to run as a younger man, in his thirties and forties, he wouldn't have guessed that he'd still be running in his sixties. He'd assumed he'd get tired of it, or his body would, and he'd retire into walking. He wasn't even sure he liked it much anymore. He'd been having difficulty tying the laces of his sneakers. This morning he'd lost his balance when trying to put on his running shorts and had to sit on the bed. His leg muscles had been cramping lately no matter how much he hydrated and stretched. Maybe he still ran for the connection he felt with Nick, and for *this:* the moment he stopped. Two miles along the Schuylkill, two miles back, and then the runner's high as he walked the final quarter mile, sweat drying on his face and back, forty-something degrees, Swish panting and happy beside him.

He liked to run early enough that there were few other runners. He'd run four miles and it was still only 6:45. A good thing, because he started laughing. He opened his eyes and checked that no one was nearby; they'd think he was crazy. He was remembering the Bush-Gore debate the night before — or, as he liked to call it, the Bush-Bore debate. It was the first time he'd watched a presidential debate since he'd been *in* one nine years earlier. He was laughing about the nod. Bush was speaking when Gore stood up and wandered closer to him. Bush gave him this nod that translated as "Hey, tough guy, you're crowding my space — you okay?" Spontaneous and brilliant from a man not at all brilliant. David knew right then that Gore would blow this. Much smarter than Bush, far more qualified, but he'd sighed like a petulant child during the first debate, and now this weak attempt to out-tough Bush by invading his space. Probably already too late. God, David was so glad to be out of that world — though of course his exit had been sudden and humiliating. There was that. He stopped laughing.

When he opened his eyes, a man stood a few feet away from him — invading *his* space the way Gore had invaded Bush's. The man was much bigger than David, tall and bearlike, with baggy, dreary gray pants and a gray sweatshirt, unlaced work boots. David noticed the man's eyes — blue with frighteningly dilated pupils — before he saw the knife. The man took a step forward so that the knife was one quick jab from David's heart. He felt his balls constrict. His breath quickened. Swish pulled, probably wanting the man to pet him. David tightened his grip on the leash. The man hadn't asked for money or anything, hadn't asked David to back up against the fence behind him. He had nothing to offer anyway: no money, no wallet, only his house key in the pocket of his running shorts.

Then, suddenly, his fear was gone. He

didn't care what happened. This might be the way he deserved to die, he thought. It would make for an interesting news story. Former presidential candidate David Christie was murdered early this morning in Philadelphia. The man hadn't blinked. Swish kept pulling on the leash, and then David knew what to do. He didn't care what happened to him, as long as the dog wasn't harmed. He dropped the leash, and Swish bounded along the path and back; he wanted to play. The man looked at the dog, and David might have run then. He was sixty-one years old, but he could outrun this man. Swish returned to David's side. The man finally blinked, his eyes filled, he looked about to cry.

And then the man walked away.

David leashed Swish and stayed where he was. He watched the man wander to the end of the path, where he dropped the knife before continuing toward Center City. David's hands were shaking, but not because he was scared.

OCTOBER 2004

Betsy kneeled on the kitchen floor. "It's all right, Dad," she said. "Let me take care of it."

She'd come home to see her father, to tell him about the man she'd been dating. His name was Cal, and he used to be one of her mother's students at Buchanan. He was a psychologist and had volunteered to help with the foundation, counseling high school students from single-parent homes. He was eight years older than Betsy — he'd been a freshman in college when Betsy was ten, when Nick died. When she met him to talk about her mother's foundation, she thought he was handsome. A buzz cut rarely made a man look handsome, Betsy felt, but Cal's made him look boyish, and he had dimples, and maybe because he'd been her mother's student, she imagined him younger than he was. The first time they met for coffee, she couldn't ask him enough about her mother. What had she been like as a teacher? What grade did he get in her class? He told her that it was strange to see her as a woman when the last time he'd seen her she'd been a girl — maybe eleven or twelve. He'd stopped by during her mother's office hours, and Betsy was there doing her homework. She didn't remember, she told him. She liked that he'd called her a woman; she liked that word, about her, in his voice. And she liked that he already knew her, in a way, through her mother, and that he knew what had happened with Nick; and certainly he knew everything else too. She wouldn't need to explain much to him.

"Really, Dad, it's okay. It's just a spill. No big deal."

She knew it wasn't just a spill.

No, she wouldn't tell him about Cal now. If her mother were alive, Betsy probably would have told her first. Then her mother would have told her father. She would have told her mother about the mud. Actually, if her mother were alive, there would be no educational foundation in her name, no summer retreat for high school students — bright kids who would be, Betsy hoped, the first in their families to attend college — and she never would have met Cal. So: *bad*

led to *good* and *good* to *bad,* and she supposed that if you lived long enough, those
words lost their meaning.

She spent most of her time in an office,
and she looked forward to each retreat in
Upstate New York — hiking and swimming
and color wars, some college advising. It
had rained the first three days of this summer's retreat, and on the fourth day, one of
the kids waded into the lake and her feet
got stuck in the muddy bottom. She wasn't
in any real danger, but she was scared, and
so Betsy took off her sneakers and waded in
to get the girl. Except she got stuck too —
she couldn't lift her feet, the mud was like
quicksand — and then she fell under the
water. She started to panic, but managed to
stand. Then she fell again.

Cal didn't strike Betsy as the outdoors
type — he was great counseling the kids,
but he was always swatting at bugs or wiping dirt from his white sneakers — but there
he was in the lake, holding her up. He held
her hand, and she held the girl's, and he led
them both out. Everyone cheered and
clapped. Betsy, covered in mud, hugged the
girl. When she opened her arms to hug Cal,
she sensed his hesitation — he was wearing
a white polo shirt — but then he pulled her
against him. After a long hug, when they

separated, his shirt was muddy. "Sorry," Betsy said. He smiled, reached out, and wiped mud from her face.

No, she wouldn't tell her father that story, and she couldn't tell her mother, except in her thoughts. She wasn't even sure she understood what it meant. Something beyond her articulation, something about her being muddy and Cal being clean and his taking away some of her dirt — maybe it was best not to understand it and just enjoy falling in love.

She wanted to tell her father, but not now. She was on her knees with a rag.

She thought at first that he'd spilled the coffee because his hands were shaking — she'd noticed — but now she saw that the mug was upside down, and he seemed to have no idea. Coffee had run off the kitchen table and onto the floor. Betsy had gotten out of the way just in time or she would have been burned.

"Shit!" her father said.

"It's okay," Betsy said, "it's okay."

"Shit!"

"It's just a spill."

"Stupid."

Her father reached down and tried to take the rag from her, but she said, "It's all right, Dad. Let me take care of it."

Ten years ago her first college roommate had asked her if she was an only child. No one had ever asked her that. The question had been in the present tense: "Are you an only child?" Well, she had been — *then.* But "yes" wouldn't come out of her mouth. It wasn't true, no matter the verb tense. She'd *had* a brother. But sometimes — now, for example, as she cleaned up spilled coffee, her father standing there with his hands in his pockets — she felt him in the present: I *have* a brother. He's here. Only a memory, someone might say. Just missing him. But it felt more than that: like the light beneath her closed eyelids, and the Nick-presence she felt hovering above her shoulder when she walked to school those first days after he died. Painfully close. And even if it *was* only a memory, even if that was the only place where they might all meet again, then so be it.

"Are you an only child?"

No, actually, I have a half sister I've never met.

"I had an older brother, but he died."

"I'm so sorry," her roommate said.

"It was years ago. He was sixteen."

"I'm really sorry, Betsy."

Her second college roommate told Betsy that she wanted at least three children —

definitely not just one. That way, she said, they would have each other to deal with their old and sick and crazy parents. "I think of my own parents," she said, "and I'm glad not to be the only one to have to deal as they get old. I mean, can you imagine?"

"I don't think of elderly parents as things to deal with," Betsy said.

"I never said *things.*" Then: "Shit, I'm sorry, me and my big mouth. You're all alone."

"I'm not alone."

"You know what I mean — an only child."

"I had a brother."

"Right, I know, but —"

"I cared for my mother when she was sick, and it was an honor."

"I didn't mean —"

"And I'd feel the same about my father."

"Betsy, all I said was I want three kids."

"That's not all you said."

"Hold on, how did we get here?"

Betsy closed her eyes and considered this. It was a great question, maybe *the* question: How did we get here? How does anyone wind up wherever they are?

"I'm being sensitive," she said. "I'm sorry."

"And I wasn't sensitive enough," her roommate said. "I'm the one who's sorry."

"It never happened," Betsy said.

"What never happened?"

"Our little argument."

"What argument?"

"Oh, I get it," Betsy said. "A joke."

But now this was no joke; spilled coffee was not just spilled coffee. She *was* an only child, and her father was shaking — not only his hands — and she did wish Nick were here.

FEBRUARY 14, 2006

The year she was thirteen. Unlucky thirteen. The year she let a boy get lucky with unlucky her. Three years older than her, but still a boy. Closer to being a man than any other boy she knew. She knew the difference. Her mother's boyfriends were men. When she used to ask her mother if a guy was her boyfriend, her mother would say, "Oh, you know, we're involved." But about one man, the year Avery was thirteen, her mother said, "I guess you could call him that." Avery didn't like to call them by name — only "your friend," "what's-his-name," "you-know-who" — except for the man her mother was dating now. Edward Plank, but her mother called him Eddie. Avery's boy, though she never called him *hers* and he never called her *his,* was Steve Hoffman, though everyone called him Hoff.

Eddie was a big guy who wore his weight

well and dressed impeccably. Button-down shirt, khakis, loafers. He wore cologne, but not too much. His dark hair, slicked back and parted on the side, was always just the right length, as if he had it trimmed weekly. He was one of the few men her mother had dated who was as handsome as she was pretty. Nice smile, striking green eyes, long girly eyelashes. He didn't blink so much as close his eyes briefly and calmly as if resetting his vision. He kept his mouth closed and breathed evenly through his nose. He owned an Italian restaurant in Brooklyn. Avery's mother took her there for her thirteenth birthday. Eddie noticed her mother, came to the table, and that was it — he was gaga.

Hoff went to the high school for gifted kids that Avery would eventually attend. He was quiet and smoked and rarely smiled and had a James Dean thing going on. Dark half circles under his eyes, torn black sweater, a tortured soul. Too cool to play sports or join clubs, too cool to do *too* well in school, too cool to have a girlfriend or best friend. He was the guy standing on the corner, smoking. He was the guy who paid for cigarettes with change. He was the guy you never saw eating. He was the guy other guys would walk up to just to shake his hand and say,

"What's up bro." Avery pretended not to be as into him as she was because she didn't want to be the way her mother had been with her father. Being crazy about someone meant that you were weak and vulnerable.

Hoff didn't seem to care who Avery was — or rather, who her mother was and what had happened. They never talked about it; others did, she knew.

It was Valentine's Day night, and her mother and Eddie were fighting behind her mother's closed bedroom door. Avery did her best not to listen, but it was impossible not to hear her mother say, "You think you're so important," and Eddie say, "You're a real piece of work," and her mother say, "I knew from the moment I met you that you were nobody," and Eddie say, "Stop being a child," and then her mother crying, and Eddie saying, "Would you *please* stop," and her mother saying something Avery couldn't make out, and Eddie saying, "Rae, please calm down," then for a while no one speaking, then her mother's little-girl voice.

Avery made sure they didn't hear her leave. She called Hoff and told him to meet her in the park where they'd sometimes go to smoke and kiss. During her walk there, she had the feeling that someone was following her. She was certain that the same

267

car — a silver Audi — had driven past her three times. The man driving the Audi wore round glasses and had long brown hair in a ponytail.

When Avery arrived at the park, she sat in the outfield grass, the usual spot where she met Hoff, and watched the Audi circle the park. The second time around it stopped near the entrance and the headlights went out.

It was too dark to see, but she heard a car door open then close.

A figure approached across the baseball diamond: the sound of dirt kicked, a casual walk, hands in pockets. The person came closer, and now she could see that it was Hoff.

She was less scared now that he was there. Even less when she kissed him and they fell back in the grass. But she became scared again when he popped open the button on her jeans, unzipped them, pulled them down below her knees so that he could spread her legs, and slid his hand beneath her underwear.

She watched her breath make dying puffs of steam in the cold air above her. After it was over, she pulled up her jeans, and then he did. They sat silently in the grass, Hoff's hair hanging over his eyes. They shared a cigarette as they walked to his car. As they kissed by the park's entrance, there was a camera flash, close, then another, and another, and the ponytailed man hurried to his Audi and drove away.

Hoff said, "What the fuck," but Avery said nothing. She made herself a promise — she wasn't sure that she could keep it — that she would not check the tabloids in the coming days. It would not be the first time she or her mother had appeared in them.

When she got home, Eddie was pounding on the front door, yelling for her mother to open the goddamn door and let him in. Hoff asked Avery if she wanted him to stay, and she said no.

Eddie saw Avery and stopped yelling but kept banging on the door.

"The neighbors are going to call the police."

"Screw the neighbors," he said.

"They call the police for every little thing."

"Let them." Eddie raised his middle finger to the world.

"What exactly do you want?" she said.

"I want her to open the door."

"It's dark inside."

"You call her — she'll let you in."

"Why are you out here?"

"I was leaving," he said, "but then she

went to the window and said things."

"My mother says things."

Avery sat on the stoop. She was sore, and her mouth was dry and tasted of cigarettes. Eddie sat beside her. She was sure she'd be sick.

"Go home, Eddie."

"Don't you have a key?"

"It's in the house." This was true, and she didn't know how she'd get in, but she would figure that out when Eddie was gone.

"What good is a key in the house?"

"Eddie — please go home."

"She can't just make threats like that."

"Like what?"

"Stupid, selfish threats."

"My mother is a passionate person."

"Dramatic."

Eddie stood and ran his hands through his hair. He buttoned his coat. "You know, I'm not like this. Your mother brings this out in me. This is not who I am, believe me."

"Good-bye, Eddie."

"I think you're right," he said. "This is probably good-bye."

He opened his arms for a hug, but Avery offered her hand. He took it, then pulled her toward him and hugged her. Her head reached his shoulders, close enough to smell the cologne he must have rubbed on his neck. The hug went on too long, past Avery's two attempts to pull away. He put his hand on the back of her head, like a father might.

"Eddie," she said, and pushed him away.

"Sorry," he said.

"For what?"

"Take care, okay?"

He walked across the small front lawn and beeped his car. The headlights flashed. But before he got in and drove away, Avery called to him: "Hold on — don't go."

She ran to the car and said, "What threats?"

"What do you mean?"

"What kind of stupid, selfish threats did she make?"

As soon as he told Avery, she took over his previous post on the stoop, banging on the door.

"Mom," she yelled at the house. "If you love me, open the door."

Avery backed away from the house and called up to her mother's bedroom window. "Mom, I need to speak with you. I did something with a boy tonight."

"What did you do?" Eddie said.

"Shut up."

"What boy?"

"Mom," Avery shouted. "I *really* need to speak with you."

"Maybe we should call the police." Eddie took out his cell phone, but as soon as he touched his finger to it, Avery knocked it from his hands.

"Jesus, Avery," he said, and picked it up. "I was just checking to see if she'd called."

She checked her phone — nothing.

"She wouldn't really," Eddie said. "She just wanted to get my attention."

"Well, I guess she got it."

His phone beeped. He looked at it, looked away.

"Sorry to say this, you're her daughter and all, and I really like you, Avery, I do, you're a smart, funny girl, you're going to be someone, but this is exactly why I told her I can't do this anymore."

"You pursued her, you know."

"What does that have to do with any-thing?"

"You were like a little puppy."

"Yeah, and right away your mother started to train me like one."

"I told you before — go home."

Without saying another word, Eddie walked casually onto the stoop, grabbed a snow shovel leaning against the house, pulled it back, and with one swing shattered

272

the pane of glass in the front door. Gently he put down the shovel. Careful to avoid the shards still clinging to the open frame, he reached inside, unlocked the door, and opened it.

They stood in the dark, just inside the house, but neither of them moved.

"Stay here," he said.

Avery grabbed his arm. "This is my house." It was strange to hear herself say this. She had never been able to think of the house as hers or her mother's because her father had paid for it. But he never visited or had any contact with them, just sent the monthly child support check.

"Let me," Eddie said.

"She's my mother."

"I'm not leaving."

She fought off snapshots in her mind: her mother in the tub, her eyes open; her mother hanging from a ceiling fan by an extension cord, a chair on its side beneath her, her eyes open.

"We don't need you," Avery said.

"I'm going to wait right here," he said.

She walked upstairs trying to take deep breaths, but all she could manage were shallow puffs, and by the time she reached the top, her arms and hands and face were tingling. The snapshots were coming so rapidly now that they became a single, constant image: her mother's eyes were open. She couldn't take this terrible feeling of anticipation any longer; she wanted whatever was going to happen to be over. She walked to her mother's bedroom and put her hand on the doorknob.

Then a calm came over her. She thought: Whatever happened has already happened — except her seeing it, knowing it. She thought: Now I won't have to worry about her anymore. And it was a surprise to admit this — that she worried about her mother.

Slowly, as calmly as Eddie had picked up and swung the shovel, she opened the door. Even in the dark she could see her mother on the floor. She was on her back, one arm at her side, the other stretched above her head.

Avery picked up the pill bottle on the floor beside her mother. She shook it and it sounded more than half-full.

Her eyes adjusted. Her mother was still dressed — jeans, a red sweater. She was still wearing one sock. Maybe she'd started to undress and gotten as far as one sock before giving up.

She moved closer and saw that her mother's eyes were closed. A dead person's eyes could just as likely be closed as open, but

Avery took her first deep breath since Eddie shattered the front window.

She pressed her fingers to her mother's neck to be sure. But Avery didn't move her mother to the bed. She wanted her to wake up on the floor and remember what she'd done. She took the blanket from her mother's bed and covered her. She took the bottle of Xanax with her.

Eddie was halfway up the stairs.

"She's sleeping," Avery said.

"Is she all right?"

"That's none of your business anymore."

He moved up to the step below the one Avery was standing on — that way they were the same height — and opened his arms to hug her.

"Good-bye, Eddie."

He lowered his arms, walked down the stairs, and left.

Avery used her phone to take photos of the empty window frame and the glass on the floor. Something for her scrapbook. Then she went upstairs to take a photo of her mother.

The photo made her cry in a way her actual mother on the floor couldn't make her.

She deleted it.

APRIL 11, 2008

Avery's mother had just picked her up from school. During the ride home she told Avery, "Sometimes I pretend that I don't know you."

"Thanks a lot."

"Be quiet, please. I'm about to say something nice."

Avery made a gesture of zipping her lips and looked out the car window at light rain falling on Queens.

"Just now, when I watched you walk down the street, I pretended you were just some girl."

"I *am* just some girl."

"That's just it — you're not. Sometimes I look at you and imagine how a stranger might see you."

"That's kind of creepy, Mom."

"I was like, who is that tall, beautiful girl? I mean, do you know you have this amazing walk where you're kind of pigeon-toed?"

"Oh, great."

"No, it *is*," she said. "You know how some models stand a little pigeon-toed — it's like that except you're walking."

"I sound weird."

"And you have a great mouth — do you know that?"

"Stop."

"Seriously, you have a woman's mouth," she said. "You're going to be a heartbreaker."

"Just like you."

Her mother was quiet for a minute. Avery was always hurting her. And her mother seemed to invite it. What she really wants, Avery thought, is sympathy. She wants someone to take care of her. Baby her.

The light rain suddenly became a downpour; it was hard to see where they were going. Her mother leaned forward in her seat and squinted. She tried to switch lanes, but a car sped up to block her. She stepped hard on the brake; traffic stopped behind her. She leaned into the horn. The sound was so loud and went on so long, Avery was afraid her mother would never stop. Her mother was shaking with rage. It was as if she were waiting for the world to say it was sorry for whatever it had done to her, and she was prepared to wait forever.

"Mom, *stop,*" Avery said, but her mother didn't seem to hear.

She lifted her hand from the wheel and stared at it. Cars behind them were beeping now.

She drove home, then parked in front of their house. It was still pouring, and they didn't have an umbrella.

"We used to play a game," she told Avery.

"Who?"

"Who do you think?"

"I don't know," Avery said. "Which is why I asked."

"Your father and I," her mother said. "We'd pretend we didn't know each other."

"Well, you didn't."

"We did."

"Not really."

"Sweetheart, will you please be quiet, just for a few minutes, and let me tell this story?" She closed her eyes, took a deep breath, and then opened them again and looked at Avery. "I know it's just a silly story to you, but please let me tell it, okay?"

"Okay."

"We're not going anywhere anyway."

"I said okay."

She told Avery how she'd stay in the Hotel Fort Des Moines one floor below David.

He didn't have much downtime leading up to the caucuses, but when he did, he'd call her room to tell her where he was going, so that she could show up too. They'd watch each other from a distance, and make eye contact, and there was something thrilling about this game, especially when they'd meet back at the hotel.

One night, a few weeks before David won the debate in New Hampshire, he and Tim Swisher went out for a beer at a restaurant in downtown Des Moines. Her mother showed up later and sat a few tables away. She was wearing stonewashed jeans, a white blouse, a black blazer, and black flats. Her hair was pulled back.

The first problem, she told Avery, was that she looked really good but David pretended not to notice her, not even when Tim went to the men's room. "It felt like a power move," she said. "You'll find out what that is, believe me."

So she broke a rule — the biggest rule. As soon as Tim came back to the table, she walked over to David.

"The look on his face," she told Avery.

She stood there smiling but didn't say anything. Finally Tim said, "Can we help you?"

She ignored him and said to David, "We

know each other, don't we?"

"I'm not sure," he said.

"You look so familiar."

"He gets that a lot," Tim said, but she wouldn't even look at him.

"I'm David."

"Rae," she said.

"Nice to meet you."

"We've met before."

"I don't know," David said.

"I never forget a face."

"Maybe you've seen me on TV."

"That's it," she said. "You're on that soap opera — what's it called?"

Tim laughed, and then David did too.

"That's funny," David said. "No, I'm running for president. That's probably how you know my face."

"I don't follow politics."

"Me neither."

"I don't trust politicians."

"Hey, I don't blame you."

"What's your last name?"

"Christie."

"Well, good luck with the election."

"I appreciate that," he said. "It was nice to meet you."

She started to walk away, but came back. "Are you sure we don't know each other from somewhere else?"

"Quite sure," David said without smiling. "Have a nice evening."

She left the restaurant, feeling embarrassed.

"I didn't like that — *quite sure,*" she told Avery now. "His tone of voice, you know."

But what David didn't know, she told Avery, was that she'd taken one of his room keys, and after his *quite sure,* she let herself into his room and took off her clothes. Her plan was to wait until David walked into the room and saw her, and then say, "Are you *sure* you don't recognize me?"

"Mom," Avery said, "do I have to hear this?"

"No, you don't have to."

Her mother looked hurt; she turned away from Avery and stared out at the rain.

"Finish your story," Avery said.

"No, it's all right," her mother said.

"Just finish," Avery said.

"I'm trying to tell you about your father."

"Go on, then," Avery said, but wanted to say: "No, you're telling me about *you.*" And as her mother continued, she imagined saying this word over her mother's story: "You you you you you you you."

"The problem was," her mother said, "Tim was in the hallway with your father. So I grabbed my clothes and ran into the bathroom just before they came into the suite. I got into the tub and closed the shower curtain."

She heard them talking about the next day — a wrestling tournament in Ames, a stump speech in Grinnell — and about the Redskins, and then the bathroom door opened. She didn't dare open the curtain to look, but then she heard David on the phone and knew it was Tim in the bathroom. She tried to think of what she'd say were he to find her. She couldn't think of any story he might believe — other than the truth. Yes, she thought — the truth. It's about time. And for a moment, a stupid moment, she considered opening the shower curtain and scaring Tim Swisher, probably make him pee on his shoes.

She thought better of it and didn't move.

Tim took forever washing his hands. When he left the bathroom, he didn't close the door. He wanted to go over a few more things with David, but David told him that he was tired, so Tim went back to his own room.

Then David came into the bathroom. She could see his shadow on the other side of the curtain. She was still afraid to move.

He pulled back the curtain suddenly, and there she was — naked.

You you you you you you you, Avery thought.

David was holding her earrings, which she'd left on the nightstand. He wasn't smiling.

"Don't we know each other from somewhere?" she said.

"We have rules."

"How do I look?"

"This isn't funny."

"What is it, then — sad?"

"Maybe it is."

"Don't say that," she said, and then started to cry.

David told her please to be quiet, someone would hear her, but she couldn't stop, and so he took her to bed.

"And then he was nicer to me," she told Avery.

"Is that the end of the story?"

"Yes, that's the end of my boring story."

"I never said it was boring."

They sat in the car waiting for the rain to stop. Avery wanted to break the silence but couldn't think of anything kind to say.

She wanted to say: "If you'd been caught that night, I might never have been born."

"I want to say one more thing," her mother said. "Make that two more things, okay?"

"Fine," Avery said.

"One, I love you — okay? Look at me."

Avery looked at her mother.

"I love you, and I'm sorry — okay?"

"You don't need to be."

"I'm sorry I can't tell you normal stories about your father — how we met, our first date, how he was right there when you were born, things like that."

"I don't need any stories."

"I'm not a bad person, you know."

"Mom," Avery said. "You don't need to convince me to love you."

"But you don't *like* me very much."

"Sometimes — I don't know, you try too hard."

"I'd like you to like me more."

"Stop trying so hard," Avery said.

Her mother stared at her for a moment. "You really are a beautiful girl."

"You said two things."

"What?"

"You wanted to say two things."

"Be better than me," her mother said. "I'm not a bad person, but please be better than me."

The storm wasn't letting up. They waited for another minute in silence, and then her mother said, "Fuck this rain." She got out of the car and ran for their front door. Avery got out and ran after her.

NOVEMBER 4, 2008

Avery knew what day it was. Every year, she started dreading it as soon as October turned to November.

Today was two days: her mother's birthday and the anniversary of Danielle Christie's death. Her mother was turning forty-eight. Danielle Christie had been dead fifteen years.

Today was also Election Day. Not that Avery could vote.

At breakfast she wished her mother a happy birthday, gave her a quick hug. Her mother sighed and said, "Two more years until the big five-oh."

Her mother looked closer to forty than fifty, her hair still long and dark, some strands of gray here and there that suited her. Avery chose not to give her even this small compliment.

But then her mother spilled coffee on her

white sweater and looked on the verge of tears. Avery cleaned the coffee on the floor while her mother took off her sweater and stood at the sink in her bra blotting the stain. Her mother's stomach was still flat, Avery noticed, and from the floor, on her knees, she said, "Mom, you don't look your age." Her mother leaned down to kiss the top of Avery's head.

On Avery's birthday, her mother stayed home from work so that they could do something together. But not on her own birthday. For two years now she had been working at a theater in Manhattan — sales, administrative work. "So what if I didn't make it as an actress?" she had told Avery when she took the job. "It's nothing glamorous or anything, but hey, you never know." Avery wasn't sure what her mother had meant by *you never know.* That she might be discovered? Given a role in a play at the theater? Her mother seemed to like her job, and today of all days it would also serve as a distraction. She never made much of her birthday and had told Avery weeks ago that she didn't want a gift.

Avery felt the weight of the day all morning and heard only fragments of what her teachers said. In math class, she worked out her own private calculations: Her mother was born in 1960, when Danielle Glass was twenty-one and in love with David Christie. They were seniors at Penn. Soon David would be off to law school and Danielle to graduate school. Four years later, they would get married, and four years after that, in 1968, they would have their first child. Of course there was no way Danielle could have known, Avery thought, that on that day in 1960, in Queens, a baby girl was born who would become the woman who would have an affair with her husband and give birth to their child. And there was no way Danielle could have known then that November 4 was the pre-anniversary of her own death. Avery, only sixteen, didn't think too much about death, but during math class she realized what should have been obvious — that the date of her own death already existed, each year it came and went like any other day. She was glad not to know. Better not to know anything about the future.

After lunch, during her free period, Avery sat alone in the library with her back to a wall so that no one could come up behind her. She put in earbuds and plugged them into her laptop. She opened her secret folder, hidden seven mouse clicks deep in decoy folders. It contained links to online videos of her father's speeches and presidential debates he had participated in, even an older debate when he first ran for the Senate, and news coverage of the scandal. She'd watched all of those many times. But one video, which she had watched only once, she clicked on now: Tom Brokaw reporting the death of Danielle Christie on *NBC Nightly News.* Today, Avery thought, you'd find out on Twitter or Facebook; you'd know almost as soon as anyone. When someone famous or even semi-famous dies, she thought, that person's Wikipedia page is updated before the body is cold. The nightly news, now, was hardly news.

On November 4, 1993, Tom Brokaw reported that Danielle Christie, "wife of former senator and presidential candidate David Christie," had died of cancer at her home in Philadelphia, and he noted that "many were inspired by her resilience under difficult and often publicly painful circumstances." He added, almost as an afterthought, that she had been an English professor at Buchanan College. The one-minute segment included a condolence quote from President Bill Clinton: "Our thoughts and prayers are with the Christie family." Brokaw ended with: "Danielle Christie was fifty-four years old." The visuals during the segment, which Avery watched twice more: Danielle's face in a box hovering above Brokaw's shoulder; a photo of their daughter, Betsy, walking between them, holding their hands; the tabloid photo of Avery's mother straightening David's tie, her face too close to his; and the blurry photo — taken secretly by Avery's nanny at her mother's urging, its authenticity disputed at first by David — of David holding Avery when she was five months old, the only time he had ever seen her.

Avery closed her laptop. She didn't quite trust herself when she made sudden decisions, but she was certain now that she didn't want to be here anymore today. What she wanted was to be seen. And heard. She was angry — she wasn't sure at whom — and sad enough that she didn't know if she could stand up, gather her things, and walk out of the school without tears. There were things she needed to say; they had been a long time coming. The angry part of her wanted to say: "Why have you never sought me out? What did I ever do to you?" The sad part wanted to say: "I'm sorry. This day must be hard for you."

During the subway ride from Queens to

Manhattan, Avery tried not to think too much more about what she might say, but it was impossible, and she was privately embarrassed at how nervous she was. "You don't know me, but —" But what? "My name is —" "I'm your — your father's —" "I know that today must be —" "I've never lost a parent — actually, my father — yours — I never really had him to lose, so —" So what? Her thoughts stuttered, and she couldn't remember why she had decided to do this, what she wanted out of it.

To be seen.

How ridiculous; how weak; how needy.

But it was true: she wanted her sister — she didn't feel that she had the right even to think that word — to look at her.

In her secret folder she had a file for each of them. Her father's contained the most information. As the train made its first stop in Manhattan, she opened Betsy's file to double-check the address of the Danielle Glass Foundation, which Betsy had started and now directed. She would be thirty-four years old — more than twice Avery's age. A few years older than Avery's mother had been when she gave birth to Avery. But in most of the photos Avery had of Betsy — from the year preceding and the year following Avery's birth — Betsy was close to

Avery's age now; they could have been sisters.

Could have been.

How ridiculous, Avery thought. How stupid.

As the train arrived at her stop, Avery took a few last looks at those old photos of Betsy, when she was just a teenager and looked sad and vulnerable. Avery imagined that they could magically be the same age — Betsy then, Avery now. She looked like someone I might get along with, Avery thought. Might understand and be understood by.

Avery's plan — not the most detailed, she knew — was to wait for Betsy outside the building where she worked. It was 3:00 PM. She assumed that Betsy hadn't left work for the day. There was the chance, she knew, that Betsy might work late, in which case Avery might have to stand there who knew how many hours. There was also the chance, she just realized, that Betsy had taken the day off; today was, after all, Election Day.

It felt sketchy to be waiting there, lurking in front of the building on Twenty-Third Street, but the nearest bench was on the corner, far enough away that she might miss Betsy. She texted her mother to say that she was going over to a friend's house after school to watch the election results and would be home late. Her mother texted back to ask which friend and how late, but Avery didn't reply. She'd figure out the details of her story during the subway ride home.

For the next forty minutes, Avery kept practicing silently, but then she realized that she was actually speaking: "You don't know me . . . You don't know me, but . . ." and just as she decided that she was crazy and that this, what she was doing, was crazy, she saw her.

A pretty woman with brown hair held back from her face walked out of the building's revolving door and stood on the sidewalk, about ten feet away from Avery, as if trying to decide which way to walk.

Avery was scared but didn't hesitate.

"Excuse me," she said. Betsy looked at her.

Avery tried to continue, but her mind started to stutter again. "I'm sorry, but . . ."

"Excuse me?" Betsy said.

"I'm sorry, but do you have the time?"

"No, sorry, I'm afraid I don't."

Betsy smiled politely, then looked away. Avery didn't move. She took out her phone and pretended to text someone. Stupid, she thought. If I have a phone, then why would I need to know the time?

Betsy's phone rang, and Avery thought: So you *did* have the time.

Do you have the time for me — your sister?

No, sorry, I don't have the time for you.

Well, technically, they both had said sorry.

Betsy looked at her phone but put it back into her pocket. A moment later, it rang again, and this time she answered.

"Hello," she said.

Avery pretended to be sending the longest text ever, but listened.

"What happened?" Betsy said, clearly upset about something. Probably someone who worked for her had messed up. Avery didn't wait to hear more; she started to walk back to the subway station.

By the time Betsy arrived at the hospital — she took the train from New York to Philadelphia to avoid rush-hour traffic — her father was ready to be released. His only injuries, the doctor explained, were a bruised hip — thank God it didn't break, Betsy thought — and a sprained wrist from when he'd tried to break his fall.

Betsy was happy to see her father dressed, sitting in a chair. He was shaking more than

the last time she saw him, in September —
another fall, that one at home rather than in
the middle of the street, and not involving a
dog and a car.

She touched his shoulder. "Dad, tell me
what happened."

"I'm sorry," he said. "You didn't need to
come."

"When someone calls and says your father
was hit by a car —"

"I wasn't hit by a car."

"The doctor says you were."

"It was the dog."

"Where's the dog?"

Her father looked confused, then panicked. "God, where's Swish? Did he get
hurt?"

"Slow down, Dad. Tell me what you remember."

"I wasn't hit," he said. "I was grazed."

"By a car."

"Right here," he said, and touched his hip.

"But a car knocked you over."

He held up his wrist, which was in a brace.
"I'm fine," he said.

"Dad, I'm having a hard time hearing
you," Betsy said. "You're practically whispering."

"I'm not," he whispered. "Where is my
dog?"

Then he seemed to remember something. "I was walking the dog," he said.

"Why, when we got you a dog walker?"

"He's old."

"The dog walker is not old."

"The dog," her father said. "When he has to go, I take him out."

"But your legs."

"They're fine."

"They're not fine."

"He's my dog, and I like to walk him. I should be *able* to. Just up Delancey and once around the block.

"Okay, but look what happened."

"I'm not sure what happened," her father said. "Somehow he got into the street."

"What street?"

"Spruce," he said. "I saw cars coming and went after him."

"Dad, you could have been —"

Bracing himself on the chair, his arm shaking, he stood. "I want my dog," he said.

The dog, Betsy finally found out from the nurse, who had heard it from the EMTs who had treated her father and transported him to the ER, had been taken by a neighbor to an animal ER because he was limping and it wasn't clear if he'd been hit by the car as well. But Swish was twelve and his limp was from arthritis. That is, Betsy thought, unless he now had a new limp from being struck by a car.

Betsy brought her father home, a short cab ride, and told him to stay there.

"Where would I go?" he said.

Still wearing his jacket, he lay on the couch and closed his eyes.

"Just rest," Betsy said. "Don't get up unless you have to."

She got back into the cab — she'd asked the driver to wait for her — and took it to the animal ER, where Swish, tail wagging, seemed very happy to see her. The vet confirmed that there were no signs of physical trauma, just the normal aches and pains of old age. Betsy paid the bill and then brought Swish outside to the waiting cab.

The driver, leaning against the cab, smoking a cigarette, saw the dog and said, "No way."

"I'll pay you extra," Betsy said.

"Sorry," the man said.

Swish pulled on his leash, as much as an old dog could, toward the driver. He sniffed the man's shoes, the bottom of his jeans. The man shook his head and then crouched down to pet Swish. "I like dogs," he said, "but I don't give them rides unless they can fit into your purse."

"It hasn't been a good night," Betsy said. "I've been to two emergency rooms."

The man laughed. "Okay, but keep the dog on your lap."

"Thank you," Betsy said, and then covered her face with her hands. She'd been crying too much lately, and sometimes she didn't know why, and often she hid it from Cal. Tonight, at least, it made more sense. She wondered if her father remembered what day it was. If not, she would be that much more worried about him. But assuming he did remember, she considered the possibility — she hated thinking this — that her father might have —

No, he never would have put the dog at risk, never would have let go of the leash on purpose.

She turned away from the driver and tried to compose herself.

"Hey, it's no problem," the driver said.

"I'm okay," Betsy said, what she'd been saying to Cal every time he asked what was wrong. "It's just been a long night."

The driver opened the back door. "The dog can sit wherever he wants."

Betsy helped Swish onto the back seat, and then she got in beside him. The driver opened the back window on Swish's side, and the dog stuck his head out the window and let the cool night air blow against his face.

When they arrived back on Delancey Place, Betsy was ready to sleep. As she was paying the driver, thanking him again, she noticed a red, white, and blue sticker on his jacket that said I VOTED.

"Shit, shit, shit!" she said.

"What happened now?" he said.

"Please wait here," she said.

"Don't tell me," he said. "Another trip to the ER."

"No, but — just promise you won't leave."

"Swear to God," he said, and crossed himself.

Betsy hurried inside with Swish, who went straight for her father on the couch. "Good boy," he said. "Actually, *bad* boy. But we forgive you, we forgive you."

"Dad," Betsy said, "where do you vote?"

"I don't remember — some church."

"Did you vote before you got hit by a car?"

"I didn't get hit."

"Did you vote?"

"I haven't voted in years."

"Well, I didn't get to vote today because I came here."

"I'm sorry."

"As long as you vote, I'll be happy. But we need to figure out where, and we have fifteen minutes."

"At a church," he said.

"The same one where we voted for you?"

"Must be," he said.

She remembered being ten — that year, 1984, when so much happened — and walking from their home on Delancey with her father and mother to a church on Spruce Street — Catholic, Episcopal, Presbyterian, she had no idea — to vote for her father. It had been in the morning, before school. She'd sat on his lap as he filled in the box beside his name, and when he was finished, they stayed there in the voting booth for a few more minutes. He had wrapped his arms around her and rested his head against her back.

Now, Betsy helped her father down the stoop. The driver opened the back door for them. She asked him to take them to Sixteenth and Spruce. "I know it's only four blocks, but we need to make it there before the polls close."

The driver got them to the church — Presbyterian, it turned out — in three minutes. "I assume you want me to wait," he said.

"Yes, please," Betsy said. "Last time, promise."

Inside the church's basement, Betsy explained her father's medical condition to the poll workers and that he was able to fill out his own ballot but might require her help in case he got confused.

He sat in the chair inside the booth, and Betsy stood beside him. She watched, unsure if he would know what to do. He picked up the pen and held it above the paper. His hand shook so much that Betsy wanted to take the pen from him and complete the ballot herself. But this was his vote, not hers — the first time he had voted in twenty years, she assumed.

She was relieved when he started to fill in the box beside Barack Obama. He took his time, but she resisted the urge to say, as if to a child: "Be careful. Stay inside the lines."

He didn't vote in any other race at the state or local level. His own former senate seat was up this year, and the Republican who had held the seat for the past twelve years was in a tight race. Betsy hoped her father might vote for the Democrat trying to unseat the incumbent, and she considered explaining this to him, but she feared that he wouldn't understand — or, maybe worse, that he would.

Her father finished with three minutes to spare, and then they went home to watch the results. They sat together on the couch, her father on one end, Betsy on the other. Betsy had texted Cal a few times during the evening to update him on her father. She called him at eleven o'clock, when Barack Obama was declared the winner, and said, "Are you watching?" and he said, "Are you kidding — of course," and she said, "Incredible," and he said, "Wish we were watching together," and she said, "Me too."

Outside, car horns blared. Neighbors came out onto their porches and banged pots like Betsy and Nick used to do at midnight on New Year's Eve. "I'm so glad we voted," she said to her father. "I mean, *you* did." But he had fallen asleep on the other side of the couch, Swish asleep at his feet.

Avery thought about telling her mother the truth — she wanted to tell someone what she'd done, how she'd felt humiliated — but she stuck with her story: she'd been with a friend. She could tell that her mother didn't believe her.

Later that night, they watched TV together. The presidential election had been called for Barack Obama, and now, in Chicago, he walked onto a stage with his wife and two daughters to deliver his victory speech.

"What a beautiful family," her mother said.

Her mother had tears in her eyes. So did many people in Grant Park in Chicago, Avery could see, but she wondered about her mother. Part of it had to be Obama — even Avery felt that she could cry — but something about the way her mother had said "What a beautiful family," it sounded part admiration and part envy.

And for once, for once, she understood her mother. Because she too felt it. Such beautiful daughters. Their adorably awkward waves to the crowd. Obama kissed them each on the head, then kissed his wife, and Avery thought: Let it be authentic. Let this family turn out to be okay.

"It's been a long time coming," Obama said, and there was Jesse Jackson, crying, and there was Oprah, crying, and Avery looked over at her mother wiping her eyes.

Before the speech was over, Avery stood up.

"Where are you going?" her mother said.

"To bed."

"Don't you want to watch?"

"I watched."

"This is history, you know."

"It's awesome, really. I'm just tired."

In her room, she lay in bed but didn't turn

out the lights. For another twenty minutes, it would be *that* day — the day her mother was born, the day someone else's mother died. From now on, it would also be the day she spoke to her sister for the first time, and the day an African American had been elected president.

She was surprised that, of all these, the one thing that continued pressing on her, just as it had at school that morning, was Danielle Christie. She shared Avery's name — part of it. Avery Bautista-Christie. Danielle Christie had been born Danielle Glass, and now in death, at least in the name of her foundation, she was Glass again. Avery wondered what it would feel like to change her name. She could become Avery Bautista, drop the Christie, distance herself from her father and sister. Or, even better, she could drop the Bautista too. Choose a new name. Leave them all behind.

■ ■ ■ ■

PART SIX:
SISTERS

2010

■ ■ ■ ■

Two wet lines from the wheels of David's wheelchair trail Avery as she walks down the hallway.

She has to hand it to Peter: he doesn't show too much surprise when he opens his dorm room door and sees Avery, dripping wet, with a much older man, also dripping wet, in a wheelchair.

She steps into his room, leaving David in the hallway, but doesn't close the door. Quietly, so that David doesn't hear, she explains what happened: the man in the wheelchair is the one she's been visiting at a nursing care facility; she was taking him out for a few hours; they were caught in a flash flood; a man who looked like Willie Nelson saved them and drove them to campus; Peter's car —

"My mom's car," he says.

"It was very sudden," Avery says. "I pulled

over, I was trying to be safe, I swear, but then the water was —"

"My mom didn't want me to have a car on campus," Peter says. "I pleaded, I lobbied, I bugged the crap out of her."

"I'm so sorry," Avery says.

"As long as no one's hurt," Peter says. "Are you okay?"

"Sort of."

"And is he okay?"

"I think so," Avery whispers. "I mean, generally, no."

"You told me he's sick."

"Which is why I need to get him back."

"Can someone pick him up? Like his family?"

"Probably not. It's complicated."

"Let me text my roommate," Peter says. "Maybe we can borrow his car."

"I'm really sorry, Peter."

She turns to look at her father shaking and wet in his chair in the hallway. "His name is David," she tells Peter, realizing then that she probably shouldn't have said this, that if anyone would recognize David Christie, even eighteen years after he fell off the radar, it would be a political junkie like Peter, and now he has a first name. Stupid, stupid, she thinks.

Peter walks into the hallway and stands

near David's chair. "Hi, I'm Peter," he says.

"Peter what?" David whispers.

"Peter Swann."

"That's a good name," David says. "Don't ever ruin it."

"Do you need anything?" Peter says to David, and when he doesn't answer, Peter looks at Avery.

"Thanks," Avery says, "but if you're able to borrow your roommate's car, that would be awesome."

In her room, waiting for Peter to text her, Avery blow-dries her father's hair. She hangs his raincoat to dry; his shirt and tie are damp, but not nearly as wet as his pants. She remembers that she still has the blue tie from the first time she visited her father. She gets it from her sock drawer, where it has been folded neatly for the past month. Carefully, she loosens the knot of the tie he's wearing until it comes undone. After laying that tie on her desk to dry, she stands behind his wheelchair with the tie from her drawer. She flips up his shirt collar and on her first try ties a perfect knot. When she walks around to the front of the chair to look, she sees that her father's eyes are closed. At first she wonders if he's sleeping, but then he opens his eyes and looks at her. "So now you know," he says, "how to tie a tie." Avery pats the legs of her father's pants with a towel, but this doesn't dry them much. She takes off his shoes and socks and then wrings out his socks into a coffee mug. She drapes the socks over her desk chair and finds a pair of her own, gray wool socks, too small to fit her father well but better than putting the wet socks back on.

Avery looks at the bed, which she intentionally left unmade. The pencil Peter gave her lies on top of his note on her desk. Last night and even this morning seem very long ago.

She crouches beside her father and says, "We'll get you back soon."

"Don't bring me back," he whispers.

"Your family's probably looking for you," she says. "And for me."

Peter helps her bring David inside. A young police officer, tall and trim, his uniform dripping wet, is standing at the nurses' station. He and Peter are wearing the same horn-rimmed glasses.

As angry as the staff are, they're also relieved to see David.

"You can't just leave with someone," the nurse with gray hair says. "You didn't sign out. We had no idea where Mr. Christie was."

Peter puts his hand on Avery's back. "No one said anything," she says. "We walked right out."

"Who was at the front desk?" the nurse says.

"I don't want to get anyone in trouble," Avery says.

"I asked her to," David whispers.

The nurse and police officer lean in closer to hear. "I wanted to go," he says.

"I'm sorry about all this," Avery says.

"You're very loyal," David says to her, and then the nurse pushes his wheelchair away.

"What's your name?" the officer says.

"Avery."

"Avery what?"

"Avery Modern."

"What's your relationship to Mr. Christie?"

"I visit him," she says. "I keep him company."

"Do you know how worried his family is?"

"I'm his family," Avery says. Peter's hand is still touching her back.

"You said your name's Modern," the officer says.

"No disrespect, Officer," Peter says, "but some people don't share their father's last name."

"Who are you?"

311

"Peter Swann," Peter says. "I don't use my father's last name either."

"Okay, but who *are* you?"

"I'm her friend."

"Let me explain why I'm here," the officer says. "A man who lives in this facility was unaccounted for, so they called the police, and now it's my job to make sure the missing person is accounted for — check — and ascertain *how* he went missing — check — and *why* — check — and if any laws were broken."

"Do you know who he is?" Peter says.

"Yes."

"And do you understand who *she* is?"

"May we leave now?" Avery says.

"As soon as I receive word that no one wishes to press any charges."

The officer asks Avery for identification, and she gives him her driver's license. He writes a few things in his small notepad, then walks away to speak with the nurse and several other staff members.

"You recognized him," Avery says.

"Yes," Peter says.

"When I brought him to your room."

"When you said his name."

"Did you know then that he's my father?"

"I searched *Avery Modern* and *David Christie,* and Google filled in the connection for me. A few more clicks and there you were."

"Do you care?"

"Of course," Peter says. "Wait, do you mean do I care who your father is?"

"Yes."

"No," Peter says. "I mean, I *care,* like I want to know about you, whatever you want to tell me, but — what I'm trying to say is that I give a shit and that you didn't do anything wrong and you're going to walk out of here with me and if for some stupid reason they don't let you, I'll stay, and if they haul your ass to jail, I'll get myself arrested so I can keep you company."

"That's sweet," Avery says, "but they probably wouldn't put us in the same cell."

"No one's going to jail." The officer is standing behind them. He gives Avery her license, looks at his notes, at his phone, and then at Avery. "You won't be allowed here," he tells her, "unless you contact Mr. Christie's family to get their permission."

"She's his family," Peter says.

"She's not listed as such in any legal capacity when it comes to Mr. Christie's health care."

"She's his daughter," Peter says. "Legally, biologically."

"That may be so, but —"

"That *is* so."

The officer removes his glasses and stares hard at Peter. "Are you auditioning for the role of boyfriend?"

"He already got the part," Avery says.

"It's good to be protective," the officer says, "but you're not helping right now."

He turns to Avery and his tone softens. "You can take this up with his family or with a lawyer, but in the meantime, please keep your distance."

During Betsy's drive through Buchanan to the nursing care facility — they called to let her know that her father is back — the rain stops so suddenly, after having poured down all day, that the silence seems louder than the rain and wind have been. Near Buchanan College, Betsy maneuvers around a downed tree limb and almost hits a delivery truck head-on. She presses on the car's horn and swears, but immediately following this adrenaline rush is a surprising calm. An accident would be okay, she thinks, as long as no one's seriously injured. It would be nice to be taken care of — physically. To be bandaged and X-rayed and splinted and sedated. But then she remembers Nick and thinks: How terrible to wish for an accident.

The nurse at the front desk explains to Betsy that her father is fine — wet, but safe.

She gives Betsy a small piece of paper with a name written on it. "This is the name of the young woman," she says. Betsy looks at the paper and nods.

She goes to her father's room and knocks.

"Come in," a woman says.

Betsy opens the door and sees her father in his wheelchair; he's wearing a raincoat. He looks at her but doesn't smile. She would like to be a child, to kneel beside her father's chair, lay her head on his lap, and feel his hand, no longer shaking, on her head.

He whispers something she can't hear; she moves closer.

"It was my idea."

"It's okay."

"I told them it's not your fault."

"Do you know who I am?"

"My friend."

"Your daughter," she says.

He stares at her. "I know that," he whispers, "but I don't remember your name."

"Betsy."

"I'm sorry," he says.

"It's all right."

"Betsy, where is your brother?"

"I don't know."

"He must be somewhere."

"He must be," Betsy says.

The nurse, a freckled woman in blue scrubs, pulls Betsy's father's arms free from his raincoat and then hangs it to dry.

"I can help," Betsy says.

"That's okay, hon. I've got it."

"I'd like to."

"You just sit and rest."

She decides to help anyway. She undoes her father's tie, unbuttons his shirt, and then pulls his arms out of the sleeves. She drapes the shirt on the back of a chair. The nurse lifts his undershirt over his head. Except for a small belly, he's still thin, his chest hairless. Betsy unlaces and pulls off her father's shoes; his socks — wool socks she doesn't recognize — are dry, so she leaves them on. The nurse removes his pants and boxer shorts, and for a brief moment, before she puts on his pajamas, he is naked except for the socks.

Soon after the nurse moves Betsy's father to his bed, he is asleep, his mouth slightly open.

Betsy asks the nurse if she can have a moment alone with her father.

"Of course, just call if you need anything."

He looks older than the last time she saw him, at Christmas, his face thinner, drawn, and yet lying in bed with the covers pulled up to his chin, he seems like a boy. Betsy moves a chair close to the bed and watches her father sleep. Then she closes her eyes and plays a game she used to play as a girl — or a version of it. In school, whenever she read about history — ancient Greece, the Roman Empire, the American Revolution — she liked to close her eyes and pretend to be a girl who had traveled centuries through time to the present — the 1970s or 1980s — and then open her eyes and imagine how astounded she would be, how bewildered and curious and a little frightened, to see cars and TVs and Atari and sneakers and to hear rock and roll and pop music, and everything she encountered, as this girl from the past, filled her with wonder and seemed impossible, miraculous. Now, with her eyes closed beside her father's bed, she imagines that she is the girl she used to be — seven or eight years old, maybe, before the accident — and has traveled forward in time to this moment. She opens her eyes: she is a grown woman, her father is old and sick, her mother is gone, her brother, gone. Those old feelings return — wonder, bewilderment, fear, the strange miracle of time passing, the relentless drive forward, the impossibility of reversal, what minute by minute, over years, becomes the stories of our lives.

■ ■ ■ ■

Betsy drives to campus and parks near Stafford Hall. She takes the stairs to the third floor and sits in the hallway, her back against an office door. If she were younger, she might pass for a student waiting for an appointment with her professor. She turns and looks up at the nameplate. She remembers being ten and seeing *Professor Danielle Christie* on the door and wishing it just said *Mom.*

The elevator door, directly across from her mother's old office, opens. A man with a white goatee and wearing a dark blue custodial uniform walks out of the elevator carrying a large black trash bag. He doesn't see Betsy, he's walking right at her, fingering a bulky key ring, and then he sees her and says, "Oh!" and steps back.

"I'm sorry," she says.

"Are you locked out?"

"No, I was just waiting for someone." She stands and steps aside.

"That's okay, that's okay," he says. "No worries."

He opens the door and goes inside. "Be right out of your way," he says. He empties a small plastic wastebasket into the large black trash bag, and Betsy has just enough time to look up and see shelves filled with books that are not her mother's, and as the man closes the door behind him he says, "Sorry, I have to lock the door," and she says, "I was just leaving. The person I was looking for isn't here," and he says, "All right, then. You have a lovely night," and she says, "You too."

She walks across the quad to the library. She knows, because she's been here with her mother, where the quietest places are. She takes the stairs down to the basement level. It's past nine o'clock, and though the rest of the library is well lit and filled with students, down here it's dark. She doesn't see or hear another person. As soon as she walks into one of the literature aisles, motion-sensor lights come on. She scans the spines: James Baldwin, Arthur Miller, Sylvia Plath, John Steinbeck, Tennessee Williams. She finds *Pet Sematary* for her brother, *All the King's Men* for her father, *A Streetcar Named Desire* for her mother, and her mother's scholarly book, *Fate and Choice in Modern Tragedy*. She carries them to the cubicle closest to the fire exit, stacks them on the desktop just to have them near, lays her head on her crossed arms, and closes her eyes.

MARCH 16, 2010

The next morning, waterlogged Buchanan, Pennsylvania, slowly drips dry. Betsy drives from the hotel, where she spent the night, to the nursing care facility, making sure to move the car carefully through standing water stubbornly refusing to recede. She turns on the windshield wipers to clear rainwater blown from trees.

When she arrives, her father is at the window in his wheelchair, his back to her. He looks to be taking in the day, or daydreaming, but when she reaches him she sees that he's sleeping: only in sleep is his body still. She sits in a chair beside the bed and waits. A nurse knocks and comes in to check on Betsy's father. She tells Betsy that he is running a fever, so it's not a surprise he's asleep. "Call if you need anything," the nurse says before she leaves.

Betsy can't help but connect the fever with

what happened yesterday — his being out in the storm and returning soaked and cold. But she knows that's just a myth, something a doting grandmother might say: "Careful out there or you'll catch your death of cold."

Her father shakes suddenly, his hands jerking up from where they were at rest under a blanket on his lap. Maybe a bad dream. Maybe just the Parkinson's. The blanket falls to the floor. Betsy picks it up, lays it over her father's legs, tucks his hands under it, gently pushes back a lock of gray hair that has fallen over his eyes. You need a haircut, she thinks. But his hair a little longer makes him look younger; even now that he's in his seventies, there's still something boyish she can see in his face. Plus, why bother with a haircut at this point?

At this point.

She's not sure what she meant by that. Mentally, she takes it back.

She can do this, she thinks. Sit with him, cover him, make sure he's comfortable. Let him rest.

She will do whatever is required, because that's what she has always done: what's required.

Except the eighty-one days since Christmas, when she last saw him.

Except not telling Cal what she should

have told him a month ago. So often the truth, which should be easy, is precisely what's most difficult to say: "I'm pregnant, but scared. Sometimes I worry that all parents, to one degree or another, mess up their kids."

She practices saying this in her mind.

She wants her father to wake and see her.

Or not wake, not yet, but know she's here.

During the first hour that her father sleeps, Betsy closes her own eyes but can't sleep. She notices on her father's bookshelf that only one book has its cover facing out; she knows the cover well. Her mother's first edition of *Streetcar.* She takes it from the shelf and returns to her chair. The weight of the book on her lap, this book in particular, is comforting; she rests her hands on its cool plastic dust jacket. During the next two hours, as her father sleeps, she reads the play her mother loved best, one of the plays her father read over fifty years ago to impress her. But rather than read the play through from beginning to end, which she's done three or four times before, she reads only Stanley's lines, his first words to his last, from "Hey, there! Stella, Baby!" to "Now, now, love." She wants to experience the play through only one perspective at a time. When she's finished with Stanley, she reads only Stella's lines, from "Don't holler at me like that" to "Blanche! Blanche, Blanche!" Then only Blanche's, from "They told me to take a street-car named Desire" to "I have always depended on the kindness of strangers." Each character's narrative arc, Betsy finds, becomes clear from only his or her words. She imagines a life story told that way — every word a person has ever spoken. She imagines a transcription of every word Nick ever said, first to last. Or her parents. She remembers their late-night conversations and fights, some of which she could hear and some of which she could not, and wonders, if a person who didn't know them could read only her father's words between 1991 and 1993, and then only her mother's from those same years, what story those words would tell.

Now she reads only the adverbial stage directions: finally, wearily, uncomprehendingly, defensively, carefully, suddenly, sincerely, vaguely, abruptly, reluctantly, sharply, dubiously, slowly, faintly, faintly, and she's oddly moved by the sound of these words in succession, as if together they make a song, tell the whole story, create a feeling she hasn't been able or willing to summon, a feeling for which there is no one name, only these adverbs, human sounds from a play she will always associate with her parents' courtship, contrapuntally, uneasily, unsuccessfully, ominously, bitterly, angrily, airily, radiantly, lightly, fiercely, wildly, clumsily, contemptuously, impulsively, yearningly, tremblingly, lifelessly, helplessly, breathlessly, feverishly, gravely —

Her father wakes; he looks at her dreamily, nervously, uncomfortably.

"It's me — Betsy."

Awake, he starts to shake involuntarily — his hands under the blanket, his head. She wants to hold him still.

"I can't tell if I'm hot or cold," he whispers.

"You have a fever."

"You're not my mother," he says uncertainly.

"Your daughter."

"I believe you." He coughs violently, his face reddens; he has a hard time catching his breath.

Betsy rubs his back, watching his face closely.

"Throw me in a tub with some rubbing alcohol," he says quietly.

"Mom used to do that when we had fevers."

"I thought it was my mother who did that."

"Maybe both our moms did."

"I'm tired," he whispers.

"You can sleep some more," Betsy says. "You can sleep as long as you want."

"Did you hear, I'm getting out soon."

A knock at the door — one of the nurses. Warmly but not *too* cheerfully, she says to Betsy's father, "How are we feeling?"

"Hot and cold."

She wraps a thin blanket around his shoulders to go with the one on his legs, and then takes his temperature, inserting a thermometer into his ear.

It beeps, and she looks at it. "Still fighting that fever."

"His breathing," Betsy says.

"I do hear that," the nurse says about the faint wheezing. "We'll have the doctor in to take a listen."

Five minutes after the nurse leaves, he is asleep again, his body no longer shaking. Betsy sits by the window, where her father will be able to see her as soon as he wakes. She listens to the violin of her father's lungs.

At the end of the day, hungry but too exhausted to eat, her father's fever not yet broken, Betsy drives near Buchanan College on her way to the hotel. Cal offered to bring her a change of clothes, to stay with her, but she said no, she wanted to be alone with her father, for now. Tomorrow she will have to buy clean underwear and socks. She can keep wearing the same jeans and sweater. Rows of campus lights, timed to come on at dark, illuminate walking paths from dorms to classroom buildings and to the library. She sees a student standing outside the bookstore, phone to her ear, a tall, pretty girl with long dark hair, and, certain it's her, she almost stops the car.

What she would say, she's not sure.

But as she drives slowly past the bookstore, Betsy sees that the girl is not her sister, after all.

The few times Cal has asked Betsy about her, she has said firmly that she doesn't want to know her or meet her — in fact, she doesn't even know what she looks like, wouldn't be able to pick her out of a lineup.

That was true then, but now would be a lie. Despite her intention never to, recently she searched Avery online and knows what she looks like, that she changed her name, and that she's a student at Buchanan. Which felt, to Betsy, when she found out, like the girl was stalking her family — or the ghost of her mother.

In her hotel room, she listens to three messages from Cal, offering again to come be with her. She texts him to say thank you, he's very kind, she loves him and knows he loves her and wants to help, but she needs to do this alone.

She wonders, after sending the text, what *this* means. What she must do alone.

Sit with her father. Remind him as many times as necessary who she is.

She lies down, planning to get up in ten minutes to change for bed, but the next thing she knows it's hours later and dark, that time between night and morning without a name.

MARCH 17, 2010

"Where is your daughter?"

Her father is in bed, covered with blankets. The nurse told Betsy when she arrived that her father's fever has gone up and there's still congestion in his lungs, and unless they can bring the fever down, he will need to go to the hospital.

"My daughter?" Betsy says.

"I haven't seen her in a few days," her father whispers.

"I don't have a daughter," she wants to say, but is afraid of confusing him, frightening him.

"It's just me today."

"I'm getting out soon," he whispers.

She leans over the bed and listens: the wheezing has gotten louder.

He was fine a few days ago, she thinks. Not fine; he hasn't been fine for years. But not this way. She looks closely at him but can't find a trace of the boyishness. His face is beaded with sweat, his hair flat against his head.

When she steps outside to call Cal, she sees her, the girl, it's definitely her this time, sitting on a bench outside the entrance.

Avoid her, Betsy tells herself. Ignore her. Pretend she isn't here.

She goes back inside the nursing care facility, steals glances at the bench. She's just a girl, Betsy thinks. I'm a grown woman. Why do *I* feel like the girl? A child who wishes her mother were here. Or her brother. A thirty-six-year-old woman seeking comfort from her sixteen-year-old "older" brother. She's already lived more than twice as long as he did. She's lived almost three times as long without him as she did with him. She's heard some say that the dead fade away over time — not forgotten, but not as insistently present in their absence. Not Nick, who still feels near. She closes her eyes and waits. Only darkness. Such a silly gesture, she thinks, to close her eyes and wait for something — that gradual brightening beneath her eyelids.

She opens her eyes. Nothing around her has changed. Nothing seems to have moved. The same old or infirm people in the same chairs. She returns to her father's room. He's awake but doesn't look up to acknowledge her. Again, she wishes her mother or brother could be here with her. She remembers, not for the first time, what her old college roommate said — that she wanted at least three kids, definitely more than one, so that they'd have each other. It would be a comfort to have a sibling now.

"Where is your daughter?"

Her father is awake, whispering to her. Again: "Where is your daughter?"

"I told you, Dad, it's just me, okay? Just me — Betsy."

Immediately she regrets her frustrated tone. Softly she says, "Do you know who I am?"

Her father opens his mouth. Betsy waits, but he doesn't speak.

"I'm not Mom — do you know that?"

She can't tell if her father is nodding yes or if it's the shaking.

"I'm not Danielle."

"The pretty girl who sits next to me in class."

"That's right," Betsy says. "I'm her daughter, Betsy."

"You look like her." Her father closes his eyes and coughs, tries to clear his throat.

"Rest your voice," Betsy says.

"Your daughter," he says.

"Dad, I think you're confused."

"Let me be confused!" She's so used to his whispering, she's startled when he yells this.

"I'm sorry," Betsy says.

"I'm confused — so what."

"Okay, Dad."

"Your daughter, the girl who comes, she looks like your brother."

"I haven't noticed."

"You should take a look."

"Okay."

"That's all I was trying to say."

Betsy wets a washcloth with cool water and wipes her father's face and neck, then presses it against his forehead.

"So what time am I getting out?" he says.

"Soon."

MARCH 18, 2010

Sometimes a mistake is just a mistake, but sometimes, Betsy thinks the next morning as she parks in the nursing care facility's lot and sees the girl sitting cross-legged on the same bench, sometimes a mistake, like driving here when you forget that your father is in the hospital — she was with him there until late the previous night — is not quite a mistake. Maybe it's a sign — but of what, she's not sure.

Did the girl sleep out here?

Either that or she went back to campus last night and returned early this morning wearing the same red-and-black flannel and the same dark blue jeans with a rip over the left knee and the same white Chuck Taylor high-tops.

She finds herself sliding down in the driver seat, not wanting to be seen, and this makes her ashamed, and being ashamed makes her angry — at the girl, at herself, it's hard to tell — and this anger is what makes her get out of the car.

She walks to the bench. The girl looks up at her, looks down.

Betsy waits, and when the girl doesn't look at her again, she sits beside her on the bench.

After a minute of silence, a long minute, Betsy says, "Would you like me to leave?"

"No," the girl says. "Would you like *me* to leave?"

Betsy waits longer than is kind to wait after such a question.

"No," she says.

Then Betsy says, "He's not here."

Avery turns toward Betsy, who is able to look at her then — really look at her face. She does see Nick; she sees him only when she's not looking for him.

"He's in the hospital," Betsy says.

"Is it serious?" Avery says. "I mean, he already has something serious, but is it something *else* serious?"

Before Betsy can answer, Avery says, "I'm a little nervous."

"He has pneumonia," Betsy says.

"This is all my fault," Avery says. "I shouldn't have taken him out."

"Being wet doesn't cause pneumonia."

"Even so, I'm sorry about the other day."

It's okay. Apology accepted. You're forgiven.

Betsy wants to say these things, but can't. Instead she says, "I'm Betsy."

"I know. I'm Avery."

"I know," Betsy says.

It's hard not to stare. Avery tries to resist the temptation as she and Betsy sit on opposite sides of their father's bed, listening to his uneven breathing, but she wants so badly to take in more of her sister's face, in person, to see if she sees herself. Betsy looks like her mother, as far as Avery can determine from having seen Danielle only in photographs. Betsy has told Avery that she looks like Nick. "Like my brother," she said. To which Avery wanted to say: "Mine too." But they never existed in this world together, not one minute, eight years between his death and her birth. She's wondered about him over the years, the Christie she knows the least about. She doesn't feel that she can rightly claim much of him as her own. And so she doesn't say, "Mine too."

Betsy, because Avery reminds her of Nick, keeps talking about him — seemingly insignificant memories that for some reason are finding her now, bringing with them powerful feelings. Like how when they were little she'd knock on the wall separating their bedrooms and he'd knock back, how this would make her less afraid of the night. How one time — the memory's foggy — there was a blackout, some kind of power outage, and a tree fell through the window, and for some reason she was naked — she was probably three or four — and in the dark her brother found her and told her everything was okay. A stupid little memory, she tells Avery, probably got it half wrong, but it's one of the most vivid she has of Nick — the feeling that he would always be with her, would always protect her.

Maybe Nick's the safest topic: the one who had nothing to do with any of *it,* what they can't talk about.

David opens his eyes and looks at Avery. "Did you hear?" He takes a labored breath. "I'm getting out."

"Where are you going?" Avery says.

"I'm finally retiring." Pause for breath. "Just me and my dog." Pause. "What's my dog's name?"

"Swish," Betsy says.

Her father seems to notice her for the first time on the other side of his bed.

He didn't ask, "What *was* my dog's name?" He used present tense, and so he doesn't remember, Betsy thinks, that Swish died a year ago. She will never tell him, she decides, not even if he asks. Maybe some things are better forgotten.

"Have you met my daughter?" he says.

"Yes," Avery and Betsy say at the same time.

He looks from one to the other, confused.

"We're both your daughters," Betsy says.

"What did I do." He pauses to breathe. "To deserve you."

Later, when a pulmonologist is listening to David's lungs, Avery and Betsy step out into the hall. "I have class," Avery says.

"Let me give you a ride."

"I have my bike."

"Please, let me."

"Thank you," Avery says, "but biking clears my head."

"What's the class?"

"It's a first-year seminar called The Lives of Others. One of those very liberal-artsy courses. Not the cheeriest material — Hiroshima, Chernobyl, Mumbai, Afghanistan, Sontag, Agee, Arbus. It should be called The Suffering of Others. It's supposed to *stretch* us, the professor said."

"Do you feel stretched?"

"Too much, maybe."

"Our own lives stretch us plenty," Betsy says.

"I don't know," Avery says. "That's one thing I'm getting out of the course — confirmation that I don't know much."

"You should get to class," Betsy says. "Go stretch."

"I'll be back tomorrow," Avery says. "If that's okay."

"One condition," Betsy says. "Let me pick you up."

MARCH 19, 2010

They see the ventilator before they speak to a doctor or nurse.

This is it, Betsy thinks — not in a dramatic, soap-opera way, and not in that way people have of overstating the gravity of a situation as a way of wishing for its opposite, but directly, truthfully, almost acceptingly.

David's doctor explains to Betsy that the pneumonia hasn't responded to the antibiotics they've tried and that her father still has a fever. She moves closer to Avery, and the doctor seems to understand that he is speaking to both of them: he looks at them alternately as he says that they plan to try another antibiotic.

Avery wants to ask questions but doesn't feel it's her place. Even though she's David's daughter, and even though Betsy has been making gestures to include her, she's mindful of Betsy's status as David's oldest — not counting Nick. Betsy's the one who knows their father best, who has spent the most time with him.

Betsy says to the doctor, a fiftyish man with a neatly trimmed beard and a soft voice she could listen to all day were he not saying the things he's saying, "Is there a chance he won't recover?"

The doctor pauses as if considering his words in a legal context. "It concerns me that the body has not responded to the antibiotics, but we will see what happens."

"But there's a chance."

"Sometimes it takes three or four days to see the desired response."

"But if he doesn't respond," Betsy says.

The doctor hasn't changed his expression or tone of voice during this exchange; he maintains eye contact, speaks quietly, factually. "The ventilator is breathing for the body right now. If the lungs do not respond, the ventilator will remain necessary. Without the ventilator, you understand, the body would not breathe."

MARCH 22–23, 2010

Three days later, David still hasn't responded to antibiotics, his fever has not come down, and the ventilator is still breathing for him.

He has *slipped* into a coma.

He has *fallen* into a coma.

As if my father slipped and fell, Betsy thinks.

He did, she supposes.

"What should we do?" she says.

"If I were in your position," Avery begins, with no idea what the second clause of her sentence will be.

"You are."

"I mean, if I needed to make a decision."

"You do," Betsy says. "We do."

"I guess I'd ask the doctor," Avery says. "I would straight-up ask him what we should do."

"Doctors don't tell you what to do."

340

"I'd ask anyway — see what he says. Say, if this were *your* father. Put him in your shoes."

"Our shoes," Betsy says.

The doctor, as Betsy expected, says that he can't tell them what to do.

"Not what *we* should do," Avery says, "but what *you* would do."

"I cannot know what I would do," he says. "I can say what I think I would do, but I cannot know. Also, you are you, I am not you — do you understand? Your father is your father. If you ask me any medical questions about your father's body, about his condition, I will give you a truthful answer."

"Is he dying?" Betsy says.

"Without the ventilator — yes."

"Are there other antibiotics to try?"

"We identified the bacterium and have treated with the proper antibiotic, but some bacteria resist. We have tried several that should have worked, but, I'm sorry to say, they have failed."

She's had the will since her father's diagnosis, a hard copy in a firebox in the house on Delancey and an electronic copy in an e-mail folder, but has not read it before now. She opens the file on her phone and enlarges the type by spreading her thumb and index

341

finger on the surface of her screen. She had been afraid to read it because she didn't want to think about her father's death and because she didn't want to see Avery's name. It wasn't about money but rather a desire to further distance herself from what had happened, and from them, the girl and her mother, the other woman and the other woman's child, to erase them even if only on paper.

But now, as she finally reads the will, Avery with her at their father's bedside, unaware of what Betsy is looking at on her phone, she sees "shall be divided equally between my two living children, Betsy Christie and Avery Bautista-Christie" and feels relieved — for Avery, that her father made this gesture, but just as much for her father, who, despite his mistakes, including not being a father to Avery, did at least this. Not nearly enough, but something.

"Do not resuscitate."

No ventilator or feeding tube "after all reasonable medical treatment has been administered and when no reasonable treatment remains or when such treatment would only serve to stay death."

Stay death.

These two words, out of context, which Betsy keeps hearing in her mind with a comma dividing them, an imperative, bring tears to her eyes, but not out of them. She turns to face the window, just in case, so that Avery won't see.

In the afternoon they meet with a hospice doctor who explains what will likely happen once David is taken off the ventilator.

They will begin the process of making him as comfortable as possible, including administering morphine, before discontinuing the ventilator. And then, as the doctor phrases it, her father will naturally pass.

It could be as brief as a few hours, or as long as several days.

He will not suffer, the doctor explains, though it might seem at moments as if he is. It will be "just the body working through its passing."

"Not *just,*" Betsy tells Avery when the doctor has gone.

A few hours later, at dusk, she drops Avery off at her dorm. "I can pick you up the same time tomorrow — unless you have class."

"It's spring break."

"So that's why it's so dead here."

"I like it this way," Avery says.

"Wouldn't you rather be on some beach?"

"I'm not a beach person."

"You don't seem like one."

"See you in the morning," Avery says.

She gets out of the car, but before Betsy drives away, Avery knocks on the window. Betsy lowers the window, and Avery says, "Do you really want to be in a hotel tonight?"

"No," Betsy says, and, imagining the long night ahead, she suddenly finally shyly quietly cries, just a little, in front of Avery.

"You should stay here with me."

Betsy wipes her eyes, rests her head on the steering wheel.

"Seriously, you can," Avery says. "There's no one here."

Without raising her head, Betsy says, "I'm so tired."

She turns off the car and gets out. Her car is crooked, the front end jutting out into the street, but she doesn't care.

In Avery's room, Betsy says, "You actually make your bed. I didn't think college students did that."

"The only place I don't mind a mess is on my desk."

The desk is covered with papers and notebooks and books with yellow and pink Post-it notes sticking out of their fore edges.

They take off their jackets and shoes, let them fall to the floor. Still dressed, Betsy gets into Avery's roommate's bed, lies on top of the covers, and closes her eyes. "I could fall asleep right now," she says.

"Me too," Avery says.

"What time is it anyway?"

"Seven something."

Avery lowers the blinds, further darkening the room, and then she gets into bed.

Betsy wakes confused. Someone is touching her shoulder, a figure barely visible in the dark.

"You're okay," a voice says.

And then she recognizes that it's Avery, and remembers where she is. She's happy to be here and not in a hotel.

"I think you were dreaming."

"I don't remember," Betsy says.

"You were knocking on the wall."

"I'm sorry I woke you," Betsy says. "Is it tomorrow?"

Avery checks her phone and sees that it's almost five o'clock. "Yes, technically."

Betsy sits up suddenly — a sharp pain in her stomach.

"Are you all right?" Avery says.

"I don't feel well."

"Are you going to be sick?"

"Yes."

"The bathroom's right across the hall — come on." Avery takes Betsy's hand and helps her out of bed. The pain comes again, like being stabbed, another wave of nausea. In the dark she can hide the pain on her face.

"Stay here, please," Betsy says. "I'll be okay."

The hallway light almost blinds her, but she makes it to the bathroom and into a stall. Let it not be that, she thinks. Not that. It would be a kind of punishment — for being so ambivalent, so afraid, for not telling Cal.

She vomits into the toilet, and the pain subsides. She catches her breath and thinks it's over, but it comes again. She vomits twice more, then dry-heaves, and then the pain is gone.

She sits on the toilet, trying to catch her breath. Then she pulls down her pants and underwear and checks: no spotting.

Thank God — not *that.* Just morning sickness.

But the fear of what it *could* have been reminds her: she wished for a miscarriage years ago. It was the only thing that might have saved her parents' marriage, and, she came to believe, foolishly, desperately, her mother's life. The birth of that child, she convinced herself, would be the death of her mother. Her mother needed all her strength to fight cancer, but the pregnancy, even more than the shock of the affair, had sapped her of whatever fight was left; Betsy could see that. And so she hoped for a miracle — a miscarriage.

But here is that baby, now a young woman, knocking on the stall door, asking Betsy if she's okay.

Betsy stands, unsteadily at first, and pulls up her pants. She flushes the toilet, then opens the door. She and Avery go back to Avery's room and get into bed.

"I feel a little better," Betsy says, looking across the room at her sister.

"My stomach is nervous too."

"It's morning sickness," Betsy says. "I'm pregnant."

"Wow," Avery says. "That's awesome."

"You're the first person I've told."

"I'm sorry you feel sick, but, I mean, congratulations."

"I don't want it to be tomorrow," Betsy says.

"Neither do I."

"I mean, I don't want it to be today."

"Me neither."

"I don't want to go through this," Betsy says.

"I'll be with you," Avery says.

"I'm not ready," Betsy says. "Can we sleep

just a little longer?"

"Of course," Avery says. "We can pretend it's still yesterday."

"Let's pretend it's a long time ago," Betsy says, and soon she and her sister fall asleep.

■ ■ ■ ■

Part Seven:
Long for
This World

1977

■ ■ ■ ■

OCTOBER 23, 1977

The wind wakes Nick. His room's dark except for a thin line of light on the far wall, sun through an open slat in the blinds. He likes being first awake, but that's happened rarely the past three years, now that he has a younger sister. She likes to hide under her blanket and call him to find her. Or to come into his room with Belly Bear — her stuffed bear with a big belly Betsy says a baby's inside — and tell Nick in the bear's imagined high-pitched voice, trying like a ventriloquist not to move her lips, "Wake up, sleepy, wake up." He's surprised she's not up yet with this wind, almost enough to frighten *him* even though he's nine and doesn't scare easily. He lies still and watches the line of light on the wall brighten. He stretches from his bed to reach the blind and flips up another slat. A second band of light appears. He turns down the slat and the light disappears. Then he twirls the wand to open all the slats until lines of light in the shape of the blinds appear on the wall. Wind rattles the window glass. Through the openings in the blinds he sees tree branches bend and red and orange leaves lifted up and up before descending onto Delancey Place, where they lift and fall again. The streetlamp in front of the house is still lit. He stares, wanting to witness the moment it goes out. He tries not to blink, but blinks, and in that fraction of a second the light goes out.

As soon as Betsy wakes, she calls for Nick. In the dark under her blanket, she tries not to laugh. She hears him come into her room. "Wait a second, I just heard something," he says. Then she feels his hands on the blanket. She squeezes Belly Bear's big belly flat, and then the blanket lifts and she shrieks. "Silly bear," Nick says. She and Belly Bear live in the Hundred Acre Wood with Pooh, her third-best friend in the world after number two, Belly Bear, and number one, her brother. Nick sleeps on the other side of the wall they share. If she wakes in the night, she knocks; he knocks back. If she knocks twice, he knocks back twice. Sometimes she knocks once and he knocks back ten times, and this makes her laugh, but what doesn't make her laugh is when she knocks one or two or ten times and he doesn't knock back at all. She will get out of bed when this happens to make sure he's really there on the other side of the wall. But he's right here, now, on her side of the wall. And with him here, the wind sounds nice, not scary — wind that could fly a kite, or lift you from the ground, then set you down again in front of your home on Delancey Place.

Danielle hears the kids, that game they play: Betsy hides and Nick finds her. It's her favorite thing in the world: to watch or listen to her children without their knowing. She can't make out what they're saying as they come down the hall, this boy and girl who were not in the world a decade ago.

They push open the bedroom door slowly. First Nick's face, then Betsy's.

"The Big Bad Wolf," Betsy says. "He'll *huff* and he'll *puff.*"

"Quiet, you'll wake Dad."

"Dad's awake," David says. He blinks, waits for his eyes to adjust to the light.

Betsy climbs into bed and sits beside him. Nick practices diving catches by lobbing himself one of David's rolled-up socks found on the floor. Betsy hides her face behind her bear and says to David in her bear voice, "There's a baby in my belly, are you the daddy?"

David widens his eyes. "Hold on now, Belly Bear."

"David," Danielle says, "is there something you need to tell me?"

"Two kids are just fine," David says.

"I'm hungry," Nick says.

"You're always hungry," David says.

"Can you make pancakes?"

"What day is this?" Betsy says.

"Sunday," Nick says.

"No, it's today!"

"*Every* day is today."

"No," Betsy says, "*today* is the only today."

"Mom, tell her it's Sunday."

"It's Sunday *and* it's today," Danielle says.

"I'm *so* hungry," Nick says.

"I saw a little black rain cloud," Betsy says.

After breakfast, David says, "Hey, an idea. Let's take a drive to Valley Forge." Danielle says, "But it's so windy." Nick says, "We're reading about the Revolution in school. Did you know hundreds of horses died here that winter? And that the soldiers left bloody footprints and died from smallpox and pneumonia and exposure?" David says to

Danielle, "And you're complaining about a little wind." Betsy says, "I wonder what's going to happen exciting today," a Piglet line she likes from *Pooh*.

Betsy, facing the window on her side of the back seat, closes her eyes and slowly rotates her head until the darkness beneath her eyelids lightens, and that's how she knows she's turned to the sun. She rotates her face the other way and the light dims again, and when she opens her eyes, there it is: her little black storm cloud.

Inside one of the log barracks Nick's been reading about, he lies on a bunk bed — a wood plank, really — and closes his eyes. Betsy tells him to wake up, but he doesn't open his eyes. She pulls his arm, his legs. She tries to pry open his eyes. She finally does, but his eyes stare straight up, expressionless. "Look at me," she says. Louder she says, "Look at me!" She takes Belly Bear from her jacket pocket and in the bear's voice says, "Please look at me," and he looks.

Mount Misery's about two miles up and back. Not too steep, more a large hill than a mountain. David and Danielle have hiked it many times, before the kids. Nick likes to lead. He finds a long stick, swings it against a tree until the stick cracks — home run. He finds another stick and stands in front of a maple tree. He swings against the tree twice without success and the third time the stick splinters — another home run.

"I'm tired," Betsy says, and Danielle says, "We're almost there," even though they're not quite halfway. Betsy says, "My feet hurt." David lifts her onto his shoulders and they keep walking. He thinks: Someday I won't be able to lift her like this, the way I can no longer lift Nick like this.

At the top, they can see the creek below, Mount Joy across the water. All the way up just to turn around, Nick thinks. Down's much easier than up. He tries to find the exact trees he hit with rocks, the exact nicks the rocks made in the bark. He tries to find the exact trees he broke sticks against for home runs and the exact pieces of those sticks along the trail and in piles of autumn leaves.

At the base of Mount Misery — so quickly they're back where they started — they walk across a wooden footbridge to the other side of Valley Creek. Water from recent storms has washed mowed grass off the floodplain, and the clippings are caught up in the roots of creek-side trees. The grass is brown and braided. A wig for a forest giant, Betsy thinks.

Hiking up Mount Joy is slower going because of the wind, but it makes no sense, Danielle thinks — maybe there's some silly superstition in this — to hike all the way up Mount Misery and not hike all the way up Mount Joy, even though there's nothing miserable about Mount Misery and nothing more joyful about Mount Joy, just the names. A silly, superstitious thought.

Nick looks for bloody footprints even though it's been two hundred years and he knows better. He looks for the bones of horses.

Sunlight comes through the forest canopy so briefly that by the time Betsy looks up, having first felt it on her face, the sun is once again shrouded by a storm cloud.

A few drops, just felt them, Danielle thinks, should probably head back down, but we're so close, might as well keep going. Besides, who cares if it's raining?

And David thinks: Rain, but who cares?

And Nick sees the ruins and thinks: No one will know.

And Betsy looks where Nick just was, on the path in front of her, and thinks: Where *is* he?

They round a bend in the path, and Betsy says to David, "Nick's gone."

"He's just ahead of us," David says.

Then he sees the stone building, really just the shell of what used to be a building, stone steps leading up to an entrance to nothing. Looks like maybe it used to be a factory, but now there's a small stream running through it. Tree branches reach through an otherwise empty window frame.

If I pull out a single stone, Betsy thinks, it will all come crashing down like blocks.

It's raining hard now, and Betsy's crying because Nick's gone, and so Danielle calls his name, they wait, nothing, then David says, "Nick, game's over," still nothing, then David in a stern voice says, "Nick, knock it off," and there he is in the empty doorframe looking like a ghost, Danielle thinks. "You've scared your sister," she says. "Come out of there. It doesn't look safe."

At the peak, they pause to listen to the rain and to look down at Valley Creek and across at Mount Misery, before heading back down.

That night, at the movies with his father, Nick decides: the second time is better. Some things about the first time are better — not knowing what will happen next, the newness of it — but overall, Nick thinks, the second time seeing a movie is better. The first time, he didn't know to close his eyes when Darth Vader choked a man with his mind, but this time he closes his eyes but can still hear Darth Vader's breathing behind his mask and the man's choking. He knows that stormtroopers will burn Luke's home and kill his aunt and uncle, and that Princess Leia will watch her home planet, Alderaan — and her parents, who live there — turned into space dust by the Death Star, and that Darth Vader will kill Obi-Wan Kenobi, Nick's favorite character, in a light-saber duel, but only this time does Nick catch that Obi-Wan *lets* Darth Vader kill him because he knows that in death he will make the Force more powerful, and this kind of blows Nick's mind, how he could have *missed* that. When the movie ends, he emerges from the theater with the sensation that the real world is less real than the world of the movie. His father says, "Let's race," and Nick says, "Okay," and his father says, "On your mark, get set . . . *go!*" and they run along Chestnut, dodging people, and just before they reach Delancey, Nick passes his father. Standing on the corner, catching his breath, his face wet with sweat and rain, Nick says, "You let me win," and his father says, quoting Darth Vader, "Don't under-estimate the Force."

Warm water running over her hand and into the tub reminds Danielle that red wine would warm her inside, would feel just right while Betsy plays with plastic mermaids and minnows and Nick's old plastic boats and the small buckets they bring to the beach, so many toys floating in the tub or sunk to the bottom, each a favorite for a month or a day, forgotten, remembered, forgotten for good, and finally given or thrown away.

She turns off the water. "Mommy needs to get something, okay?"

Betsy, happy, doesn't seem to hear or care.

"Honey, you remember what Mommy said about not putting your head under the water and not standing?"

Betsy, her face behind one of her mermaids, says yes in Belly Bear's voice even though Belly Bear's sitting on the closed toilet seat.

"Betsy, look at me."

She peeks from behind the mermaid.

"Tell me you heard."

"I heard," she says.

Danielle goes downstairs to get a wineglass and the bottle of wine on the kitchen counter. With the sharp tip of the corkscrew's worm she cuts the foil over the cork, peels it off in one satisfyingly large piece, pushes the worm into the cork, starts to twist, calls up, "Betsy, you okay?"

No answer. No sound of water play. No sound of Betsy talking as herself or as Belly Bear or as any of her toys.

She calls up again, "Betsy?"

Silence.

And then a cold feeling in her stomach as she hurries upstairs. "Betsy?" she says. She almost drops the bottle as she reaches the bathroom. Betsy is out dripping wet to get Belly Bear and bring her into the tub even though they've been over this how many times, the water would hurt Belly Bear's stuffing, but Danielle's so happy to see that Betsy's okay that she can't be angry.

The wine in her glass isn't quite half gone

when Betsy says, "Can we do double tubble?"

"Not tonight. Mommy just wants to sit here and relax."

Betsy's quiet for a moment. Then she says, "But you don't do double tubble with Nick anymore because he's too big and tomorrow I'll be too big."

Danielle laughs. "Not tomorrow you won't be — don't worry."

"Then when I'm four."

"Not when you're four or five or even six."

"But when I'm old."

No, Danielle thinks, you must never grow old. She wants to stop time right now or somehow shrink Betsy and hide her from time in the palm of her hand or back in her belly.

Danielle sets her wineglass on the floor. She takes off her sweater, and Betsy squeals with delight. Pants, shirt, socks, bra, underwear, she undresses, steps into the tub, the water still warm enough, and sits across from her daughter. She washes Betsy's feet, and Betsy washes hers. Danielle is already nostalgic for this moment, she's *pre*-nostalgic — what's the word for that, she thinks, one of those untranslatable German words. Probably somewhere in her notes. She stops washing Betsy and tries to think of the word. She considers getting out of the tub and hurrying down the hall to grab her notebook. But then she feels Betsy's hand on her leg and returns to the moment. How silly, she thinks, to want the notebook *now,* and all for a German word to describe what she's feeling. She washes Betsy's back, trying to re-create the feeling she fears she's lost by making it more than it was, when what it was was more than enough.

The lights flicker but stay on. Should probably finish washing Betsy now, she thinks, in case the power goes out. She reaches for her wine, but just as her hand touches the glass she hears a loud crash, which sounds as though it came from somewhere in the house. Startled, she jerks her hand. The rest of the wine spills, the glass breaks.

David tells Nick to stay downstairs. He takes the stairs two at a time to the second floor, where he finds Danielle in the hallway holding a naked dripping Betsy. Danielle's robe, missing its belt, is open enough for David to see that she's naked beneath it.

"We have a tree in our house," she says.

"You can come up," David calls to Nick. He hugs Danielle and Betsy. "I saw that it went right through the window by the rocker, and I thought —"

"We're okay," Danielle says.

Nick, now upstairs, says, "Will I have school tomorrow?"

"Of course," Danielle says. "There are snow days but no such thing as a *tree* day."

They walk across the hall to look at the damage. The window is gone, broken glass all over the floor. A large tree limb extends through the window frame and drips rainwater onto the floor. Wind blows more rain into the room. The rocking chair is on its side, one of its rockers in two pieces beside it. The lights flicker again, and again they stay on.

Danielle watches Nick watch David. He wants to do everything David does, wants to *be* him. David picks up the large shards of glass, then sweeps the rest. Everyone else, he says, has to stay away. With a handsaw, like the one he uses at the Christmas tree farm every December, David cuts the tree limb into smaller pieces, then drops the pieces to the sidewalk below, making sure no one's walking past. No one's coming out on a Sunday night to replace a window, so he gets a tarp and tape from the basement and cuts the tarp into a square slightly larger than the window frame. Nick's desperate to help, and so David lets him be in charge of taping the tarp, which David holds in place. Danielle holds sleeping Betsy, her robe closed to keep out the cold and damp.

Later, Nick wakes afraid after a bad dream he can't remember. He walks slowly across the hall, tries not to creak the floor. He sits at the top of the stairs. On the wall beside the staircase he sees the reflection of flickering TV light. *All in the Family* ends — he knows the song even though he isn't allowed to watch the show — and then . . . more music, the *ABC Sunday Night Movie,* which he's allowed to watch only during the summer and if the movie's appropriate for kids, but usually it isn't. He wonders, as he always does when on the stairs listening to his parents watch TV, if they know he's there.

"Do you think he fell asleep on the stairs?" Danielle whispers to David, and David says, "Probably."

And then everything goes dark — the TV, the lamp on the end table beside the couch, the sconces in the dining room, the light at the bottom of the stairs.

They hear Nick trying to find his way, then Betsy crying. "I'm here," Nick says in the dark. By memory he feels his way to Betsy's room and to her bed, bangs his foot on her dresser, reaches for the sound of her crying, takes her hand. "Don't worry," he says. He leads her out of her room and into the hallway, where they wait in the dark.

A circle of light appears on the wall at the top of the stairs. It starts big and shrinks as the source of the light — the flashlight David's holding — moves up the stairs and closer to its projection on the wall. Danielle has a flashlight too.

"You guys okay?" David says.

"Sure," Nick says as if he's never been afraid.

Danielle picks up Betsy and smells on her neck the bath they took. Betsy smells on her mother's neck her father.

"Power's out," David says. "Not much we can do but wait, but it's late anyway, so how about we call this day a day?"

"Can we have a sleepover?" Betsy says.

"Of course," Danielle says. "You too, Nick."

Nick's old enough not to want to show how excited he is about not sleeping alone.

Betsy says, "Now we can all dream together."

The temperature is supposed to drop into the thirties overnight, and there's no heat, so they lay four blankets on the bed and get under them, David and Danielle on the ends, Betsy and Nick beside each other in the middle.

Betsy asks if the light's going to come back on in the morning, and Nick says, "Even if not, the sun will come up."

Betsy yawns, then closes her eyes. The dark beneath her eyelids is even darker than the dark everywhere else, but she makes sure one foot's touching Nick.

"Can't we go back to page one and do it all over again?" she says.

Danielle doesn't know what Betsy means, but then she remembers this is a question Pooh asks near the end when saying good-bye to Christopher Robin.

Betsy tries to stay awake in the dark, but her eyes keep closing. She doesn't want to fall asleep. She doesn't want anyone else to fall asleep either.

"I want today again," she says.

"Today happens only once," Nick says.

ACKNOWLEDGMENTS

Novels are not written alone — not by a long shot. Sure, a writer works alone for a time, often a long time, but eventually, when he's done all that he knows to do, he loosens his grip on a book that no longer belongs to him and maybe never did in the first place. The novel becomes collaborative: kind, smart people show the writer that he can do more and better than he thought he could. The writer's name may go on the cover, but other names belong beside his. Here are some of those names:

Many thanks to my agent, Kim Witherspoon, and her team at InkWell Management, especially William Callahan. Just as many thanks to my editor, Meg Storey, who knew better than I did what this novel wanted to be, and to everyone at Tin House. I'm grateful to Franklin & Marshall College for funding that supported the writing of this book. I couldn't have written this novel without Richard Ben Cramer's *What It Takes: The Way to the White House,* his masterpiece about the 1988 presidential campaign.

Last but never least, let me acknowledge not for the first time how much I owe to my wife, Nicole Michels, and to our son, Dangiso.

This novel contains brief quotes from the following: John Guare, *Six Degrees of Separation* (Vintage, 1990), Tennessee Williams, *A Streetcar Named Desire* (New Directions, 1947), Maurice Sendak, *Very Far Away* (Harper & Brothers, 1957), Dr. Seuss, *The Shape of Me and Other Stuff* (Beginner Books, 1973), Ruth Krauss, *The Cantilever Rainbow* (Pantheon Books, 1965), and A. A. Milne, *Winnie-the-Pooh* (Methuen & Co. Ltd., 1926).

The jokes on page 155 are variations of jokes told by Jay Leno and Jon Stewart.

ABOUT THE AUTHOR

Nicholas Montemarano is the author of two previous novels, *The Book of Why* (2013) and *A Fine Place* (2002), and a short story collection, *If the Sky Falls* (2005), a *New York Times Book Review* Editors' Choice. His short stories have been published in *Esquire, Tin House, Zoetrope: All-Story, The Pushcart Prize,* and elsewhere, and have received special mention in *The Best American Short Stories* four times. He is the recipient of fellowships from the National Endowment for the Arts, the Mac-Dowell Colony, Yaddo, and the Bread Loaf Writers' Conference. Montemarano grew up in Queens and now lives in Lancaster, Pennsylvania, where he is a professor of English at Franklin & Marshall College.